LIFE & TIMES
ON
Pleasant Pond

LIFE & TIMES
ON
Pleasant Pond
ISLAND FALLS, AROOSTOOK COUNTY, MAINE

SANDRA S. NEWMAN

Van de Bogart
PUBLISHING

Also by Sandra Newman
Scooter the Purple Mogul Mouse and All His Mogul Mouse Friends

P U B L I S H I N G

info@onpleasantpond.com
www.onpleasantpond.com
www.vb-publishing.com

Book produced by Sea-Hill Press, Ltd.
P. O. Box 60301, Santa Barbara, CA 60301
www. seahillpress.com

Publisher: Greg Sharp
Editor: Cynthia Sharp
Book Designer: Judy Petry
Cover Designer: Tricia Orcutta
First Edition
ISBN: 978-0-615-36610-4

Printed in Hong Kong

To Mom and Dad,
for purchasing the camp, and to all the "pond people"
who make Pleasant Pond so very special.

▲ *Aerial view of Pleasant Pond (Courtesy of Richard Armstrong)*

▲ *Barker Rocks (Photo by Sandra Newman)*

Contents

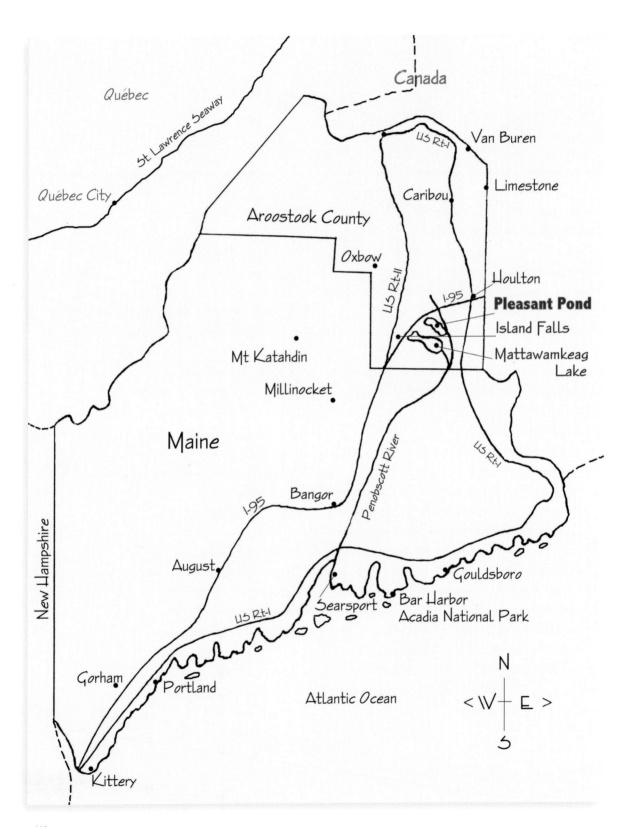

Preface

Pleasant Pond is located in Maine's northernmost county, Aroostook, in the small town of Island Falls. The county borders the Canadian provinces of Québec and New Brunswick. As the largest U.S. county east of the Mississippi River, it is larger than the combined states of Connecticut and Rhode Island. Aroostook comes from the Native American word meaning "beautiful river." The county is nicknamed the "The Crown of Maine" partly because of its geographic location and breathtaking beauty. Aroostook is known as "The Last Frontier of the East," but most affectionately it is called "The County." Northern Maine instills memories never to be forgotten.

To give you some perspective as to the location of Island Falls, this town of 760 residents is 30 miles west of New Brunswick, Canada, and 80 miles north of Bangor, Maine. The nearest town is Houlton. If you want to see a movie, you have to drive to Houlton, 27.84 miles north. Island Falls is closer to Québec, Canada, than it is to Boston.

Just south of Island Falls, I-95 Exit 244, is Baxter State Park and Mount Katahdin, the tallest peak in the state of Maine at 5,267 feet and the end of the Appalachian Trail: the continuous footpath that goes between Mount Katahdin in Maine and Springer Mountain in Georgia, a distance of about 2,175 miles. Hopefully, after reading *Life and Times on Pleasant Pond*, you will visit.

For those who wonder if Island Falls is the top end of the country, I can tell you that it is pretty darn close. If you were to drive north at the beginning of U.S. Route 1 in Key West, Florida, and continue on for about 2,377 miles, you would arrive in Fort Kent, the end of the road and the United States International Border of New Brunswick, Canada. The end of U.S. Route 1 in Fort Kent is 155 miles north of Island Falls. Traveling to northern Maine you might consider the opportunity to try out for the United States biathlon team, whose World Cup training camp venue is in Fort Kent, Maine.

Just remember, do not be tempted to take Aroostook Scenic Highway Route 11—you might see a few moose, but, unfortunately, you will miss Island Falls!

▶ *Island Falls*
welcome sign

Acknowledgments

This book has been a long time in writing, and consequently I owe great thanks to many people. Special thanks to Ted and Mary (Hathaway) Sherwood, the Hathaway Family, Ralph and Valerie (Lake) Powers, Pam (Hillman) Oliver, Anne Melanson, Pastor Mike and Linda Kasevich, and Sandy Swift for allowing me stay with them while writing this book. They all somewhat willingly listened to the many times I said, "listen to this," "how does this sound," and "you won't believe this one."

To Becky (Joy) Drew who patiently edited through e-mails, searched the Island Falls Historical Society for pictures and bits of information, and let me stay late at the Katahdin Public Library; to Linda Kasevich for reading every single page, and staying up late a few nights seeing the wee hours of daylight with me, giggling like sisters, while she responded to, "Linda, help! How do I do this?"; to Joanne Melanson for her technical critique and advice; to Sally (Walker) Cyr for her sisterly encouragement and praise; to Pete Peterson who read every single word and rewrite and still added his two cents. Thank you all!

To Joe Edwards, thank you for the hours spent sharing your stories and making me write them down, and to the Edwards Family for agreeing to my using Ralph and Keith Edwards' stories and memories. To Philip and Averill Powers for sharing your family stories and allowing me to print them.

To my dad, Dr. Newman, and his friend, Charlie Valleau, who both tirelessly let me read and re-read this book over and over to them. I miss you, Charlie.

And to all my friends who encouraged, helped, and supported me through this project: thank you so much. I did it, and here it is!

—SANDRA S. NEWMAN

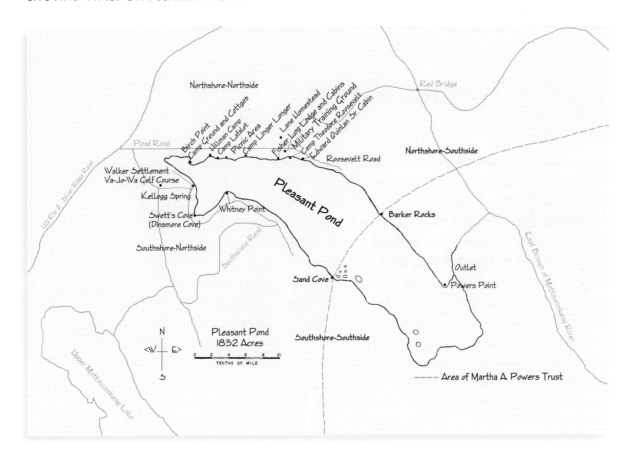

Northshore-Northside

Red Bridge

Birch Point
Camp Ground and Cottages
Hillman Camp
Camp Lafalot
Picnic Area
Camp Linger Longer
Lane Homestead
Fisher Log Lodge and Cabins
Military Training Ground
Camp Theodore Roosevelt
Edward Quinlan Sr. Cabin

Pond Road

Roosevelt Road

Northshore-Southside

Walker Settlement
Va-Jo-Wa Golf Course

Kellogg Spring

US Rte 2 - Silver Ridge Road

Swett's Cove
(Dinsmore Cove)

Whitney Point

Pleasant Pond

Barker Rocks

East Branch of Mattawamkeag River

Southshore-Northside

Southshore Road

Outlet
Powers Point

Sand Cove

Southshore-Southside

Upper Mattawamkeag Lake

N
W E
S

Pleasant Pond
1832 Acres

0 2 4 6 8 10
TENTHS OF MILE

— — — Area of Martha A. Powers Trust

Introduction

Life and Times on Pleasant Pond started when Joe Edwards requested that I write his family story, and I agreed wholeheartedly. From there, this project grew to be much bigger than I ever imagined. While I believe there is much more information to be discovered and shared, and there are more stories to be told, there comes a time when a project has to have a deadline. My friends have said, "Enough already!"

Having grown up in Island Falls, I love spending my summers in this little town and kayaking on the pond that I will always consider home. In 1965, my dad, Dr. R. Calvin Newman, the town veterinarian, and my mom, Joy (Skinner) Newman, purchased our camp on Pleasant Pond from Hope Hawks. Every summer we packed up, and happily joined the families who also packed for their annual move to either the pond or the lake.

If you ask anyone in town, Pleasant Pond is called a pond because it is entirely spring fed. With no inlet, only an outlet, it is referred to as "the pond." Lakes have both an inlet and outlet: Mattawamkeag is known as "the lake."

A cottage on Pleasant Pond or Mattawamkeag Lake might have been built with the idea of summer residency and may have included a fireplace, kitchen, bathroom, bedrooms, living room, and possibly a porch or deck, whereas a camp or cabin started out as a rustic building intended for day use or weekend use only. On Pleasant Pond, the terms have become interchangeable. Many camps have since been converted into year-round homes, but there are still many people who arrive in the spring and leave in the fall—when school starts or when it begins to snow.

In this beautiful outdoor recreation town, there is a marvelous flower shop, a grocery store that has everything you need, a lawyer, a library, and a wonderful historical society in the Old Jail House. There are three shops in the area that sell beautiful local handmade crafts. For such a small area, there are many talented artists. The area hospital might be a drive (about 28 miles), but there is a medical office. We had a veterinarian for sixty years, who at the young age of 83 decided to retire as the oldest practicing veterinarian in New England. We have restaurants that serve delicious food with delectable fish fries every Friday night. What more could a person want?

The Honorable Mr. Wiggins (Senator in the Maine State Legislature) wrote in his account, *The History of Aroostook County*, "in the whole of Aroostook County there is no more picturesque town than Island Falls and none where the natural scenery is more beautiful." He commented it was a sportsman's paradise. During the late-1800s, it was to become known as such and remains so to this day. With the many lakes, fresh-water ponds, and natural springs winding through the wooded hills, the summers are gorgeous and the winters are perfect for outdoor sport. The Penobscot and Passamaquoddy Indians Tribes were the area's first inhabitants; they spent part of the year hunting and fishing the area's many waterways.

Levi Sewall and Jesse Craig were the first settlers of Island Falls. They had heard stories of an area on the West Branch of the Mattawamkeag River with magnificent falls that supposedly swept madly through a rocky gorge and dashed over precipitous ledges. Trekking through the woods in 1843, they found this beautiful place between Patten and Houlton, and named the area after the falls that surrounded the island. Settling the area, they started to fell trees and clear the fertile soil while the Indians continued to enjoy the waters of the lakes, ponds, and rivers. With more and more settlers moving to the area, the settlement town incorporated as the Town of Island Falls in February 1872.

In 1878, Theodore Roosevelt discovered Island Falls and the surrounding area when he became a lifelong friend of William Sewall. It was this friendship that brought Roosevelt to Island Falls three times. Roosevelt visited the Sewall's home and stayed in their hunting camp on Mattawamkeag Lake. Bible Point State Park, located near the south end of Mattawamkeag Lake, is dedicated to President Roosevelt. If you hike there, you will see the plaque commemorating Roosevelt's love for this beautiful point—the point he reportedly hiked to daily to read his bible. It was President Teddy Roosevelt and Maine's former Governor Llewellyn Powers who started preserving the woodland area around Mattawamkeag Lake and Pleasant Pond: the maple, beech, birch, hemlock, spruce, fir, pine, cedar, and juniper trees within the towns 22,040 acres. With all the hemlock

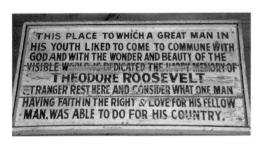

THIS PLACE TO WHICH A GREAT MAN IN HIS YOUTH LIKED TO COME TO COMMUNE WITH GOD AND WITH THE WONDER AND BEAUTY OF THE VISIBLE WORLD IS DEDICATED THE HAPPY MEMORY OF THEODORE ROOSEVELT STRANGER REST HERE AND CONSIDER WHAT ONE MAN HAVING FAITH IN THE RIGHT & LOVE FOR HIS FELLOW MAN, WAS ABLE TO DO FOR HIS COUNTRY.

▲ *On display at the Emerson Store in Island Falls*

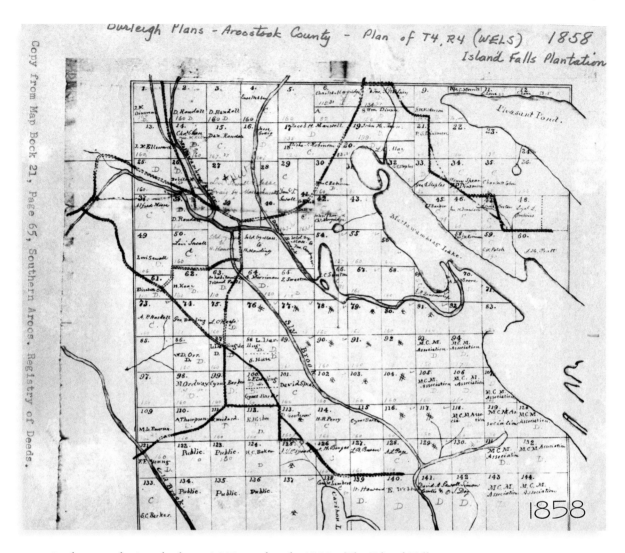

trees in the area during the later-1800s and early 1900s, The Island Falls Proctor & Hunt Company became the largest tannery in New England, processing 1,600 sides of leather per day.

Cyrus Barker and his son, Addison, moved to Island Falls in 1853 from down Maine, Kennebec County, and settled on one of the most beautiful ridges in Aroostook County just south of town on U.S. Route 2, Barker Ridge. When Cryrus died in 1886, he left the farm to his son, Rodney, who made it into one of the finest farms in the county. Today, the Barker Ridge Farm is owned by Pat Emerson, the same delightful lady who burned down her Uncle Delmont's camp, Camp Linger-Longer, on Pleasant Pond.

Robinson Mountain overlooking Mattawamkeag Lake is named after George F. Robinson. This is where May Mountain ski area had operated for many years before it closed down due to a lack of snow. It seems George was instrumental in saving Secretary Seward's life the night President Abraham Lincoln was shot, April 14, 1865. Robinson grew up in Island Falls and went on to become paymaster in the United States Army.

At one time, Island Falls and Aroostook County were part of the state of Massachusetts. In 1837, Maine's legislature dispatched an army of 200 men to Aroostook County and unilaterally declared war against Britain. The county was officially established in 1839 when it was set off from Washington and Penobscot counties. The signing of the Webster-Ashburton Treaty on August 9, 1842, marked the end of unofficial fighting of the bloodless Aroostook War. Having once been part of Massachusetts, Maine is the only other state that celebrates Patriots' Day, April 19. Celebrated on the Monday nearest the date, Patriots' Day is also opening day for the Boston Red Sox and the running of the Boston Marathon.

The time for momentous events has not come to an end for northern Maine. At the end of their 2003 summer tour, the band Phish held their first summer festival in four years, when they returned to Loring Air Force Base, Limestone, Maine. Their first concert in Limestone was *The Great Went*, which took place August 1997. The 2003 festival drew crowds of over 60,000 fans, once again making Limestone one of the largest cities in Maine for a weekend. When the anxious fans arrived at the Maine border in Kittery, they discovered they had another 367 miles on the road—about 6 more hours. With Island Falls a mere 265 miles from Kittery, many of the fans stopped in the town that greets visitors from every part of the country with a warm-hearted welcome.

Traveling around Pleasant Pond, you will discover a bowling alley at Birch Point Campground and Cottages. Taking a sharp right off the Pond Road, you will encounter the tricky 18-hole Va-Jo-Wa Golf Course—once a cow farm and still with the reputation of having an excess number of cow ponds for your golfing and ball-losing pleasure.

Our pond may be small, but it is our magical pond: our Pleasant Pond. The last chapter of my book includes stories written by my friends who live or play on the pond. I hope all the people who contributed and all who read this realize just how special Pleasant Pond truly is. Special thanks to the Powers Family for maintaining the Powers Trust and protecting what we all hold so dear. Thanks to everyone who lives and plays on "our pond" for keeping it our special place: our small but magical Pleasant Pond.

CHAPTER 1

The Settlements on Pleasant Pond

THE BARKER RIDGE FARM TO LANE HOMESTEAD

The Barker Ridge Farm, located south of Island Falls, Maine, on U.S. Route 2, played an instrumental role in the lives of four men when they arrived in Island Falls in 1858: Cornelius Lane, Francis Dinsmore, and Cyrus Barker built the Barker Ridge Farm, and Alfred Moore later managed the farm. Nina Sawyer wrote in her book, *A History of Island Falls*, that the farm was built on "one of the most beautiful ridges of land in Aroostook County," and The Honorable Edward Wiggins mentioned in his book, *History of Aroostook*, the Barker Ridge Farm was considered, at the time, "one of the finest farms in Aroostook County." Roswell Emerson would later own the farm in 1916. It was Roswell's father, Delmont Emerson, who built Camp Linger-Longer on Pleasant Pond, about 1907.

▲ *Barker Ridge Farm, 1916*
1853—Cyrus Barker
1886—Rodney Barker
1916—Roswell Emerson
1983—Pat Emerson
(Courtesy of Island Falls Historical Society)

▶ *Camp Linger-Longer (Courtesy of Island Falls Historical Society)*

AUGUST 21, 1913—
Mr. and Mrs. Delmont Emerson entertained 100 friends at their camp on Pleasant Pond Monday evening. Music was furnished by McClure's orchestra of Patten. A pleasing novelty was furnished the guests when the host and hostess substituted for the violinist and pianist in the orchestra.

—SAMUEL R. CRABTREE
News Items

Roswell and Bertha's daughter, Pat Emerson, lives on the Barker Ridge Farm today. Pat especially loves sharing her memories and stories of Camp Linger-Longer. One of her favorite stories is the one that tells how she and her friend burned down the camp.

According to the Honorable Edward Wiggins, when Cornelius Lane moved to Island Falls his mind was set on finding his imagined ideal location in Aroostook County. It was while working for Cyrus Barker that Cornelius met Francis Dinsmore, who just happened to live on Pleasant Pond, Lot 21, now Dinsmore Cove (Swett's Cove), and a long-lasting

Her grandparents, Myra and Delmont Emerson, owned Camp Linger-Longer, and Pat claims it might have been the oldest camp on the pond if she hadn't burned it down.

"Oh, I remember the pond. We owned Camp Linger-Longer, and I burned it down! My buddy, Barb, and I went snowshoeing into camp one day and saw that the roof of the camp had caved in from too much snow. Thinking the camp was beyond repair, I put a match to it and left before it had completely burned. With the snow on the roof melting, we figured it would put out the fire. We snowshoed back out to Flo Walker's, where we had started, and saw my brother, Frank, who worked for the Forestry Service at the time. I told Frank to go check the camp because I might have burned it down, telling him there was too much snow on the roof, it had collapsed, and all. He hikes in, and when he comes out, you know what he said? 'There is not a God damn thing left.'"

"Oh I did," Pat told me with a giggle, "I burned the camp down!"

—PAT EMERSON

friendship developed. It was through this friendship that Cornelius discovered Pleasant Pond: both men were grateful for the area's soul-searching solitude and appreciated the pond's magnificent natural beauty, the area's range of rolling hills, and the abundance of fresh spring water. With Francis' help, Cornelius built himself a sturdy raft for the main purpose of poling around the pond searching for "his perfect spot." Discovering a small cove midway down the pond, on the north side of the south shore, Cornelius purchased Lot 12 in Island Falls and constructed a rustic log cabin. Lot 12 was one of the three parcels of land, on the north side of the pond that Cornelius and his brother, Charles, purchased from The Honorable Parker P. Burleigh. Burleigh was one of the pioneers of Aroostook County, a land surveyor at the time who owned large tracts of land in the county, including Island Falls. In 1861, Cornelius purchased an adjoining piece of property from Burleigh, Lot 64, in Dyer Brook and cleared 12 acres before he started construction of his future home.

When the Civil War was raging, and the country was crying out, Cornelius felt duty-bound, as many men did during that time, and left his "perfect spot." He left behind his home's very impressive stone foundation, a foundation built from granite extracted from the quarry in the rear of his property. For many years natural granite was quarried around Pleasant Pond: the brook behind Camp Roosevelt, the hills on the Walker Settlement, and Lane Hill. This granite was used for the foundations of many of the area's most prominent buildings, including the Congregational Church, the Sewall House, and Delmont Emerson's home.

▲ Lane Homestead, 1861 (Courtesy of Island Falls Historical Society)

JANUARY 20, 1905—
A party of about 30 drove to Pleasant Pond Tuesday evening and partook of a old-fashioned hulled-corn supper at the home of Mr. and Mrs. Lane by invitation of Mrs. John Lane and Mrs. Harriet Edwards. A good time was had by all.
—SAMUEL R. CRABTREE
News Times

◄ Mr. and Mrs. Lane, Cornelius and Cordelia (Courtesy of Marion Hoar)

Mustered out of service in December 1865, Cornelius returned to his woodland home and completed construction in 1865. It was after Cornelius and his wife, Cordelia, moved into their home that the Lane Homestead became a favorite place for many social gatherings. On this perfect spot, they raised their six children: Charles, Albert, John, Mary, Edwin, and Lucy. Their son, John H. Lane, who was born in 1868, inherited the homestead upon his parents' death. Eleven children were raised on the homestead: four sons (who have passed away) and seven daughters (three have passed away. Marion (Lane) Hoar, who lives in Island Falls, is one of the daughters and remembers much activity around the home, including playing with Ed Quinlan Jr., whose father, Edward Quinlan Sr., purchased the property in 1960.

FROM A LANE GRANDDAUGHTER'S DIARY:

May 31, 1906—Gramp, Gram moved into cottage on the pond
July 24, 1906—Myra and Roswell boarded at Lane's
December 10, 1906—Granite from Lane's to Emerson
September 3, 1907—Benjamin Walker died, member of 2nd
Maine Calvary

▼ *Benjamin R. Walker, Pvt. Co. H. 2nd Maine Calvary, with his wife, Genevre (Courtesy of Island Falls Historical Society)*

THE CIVIL WAR AND AFTERMATH

Many early settlers living on the pond met the country's call during the Civil War and left to fight: Alfred Moore, 18th Regiment; Benjamin Walker, Company H, 2nd Maine Calvary; Charles Moore, 8th Regiment, died in Andersonville Prison; Cornelius Lane, Company A, 8th Regiment Corporal; Joseph Edwards, Company E, 19th Maine Regiment, served at Gettysburg at the high-water mark of the Confederacy, the Picketts Charge; and the Dinsmore brothers: Eben, Joshua, and Pembroke, all Company A, 18th Regiment.

The brave men who returned lead various lives: Joshua, wounded during the war, May 20, 1864, later died of a shotgun wound while shooting a rat; Pembroke moved to California several years later; Eben became involved in the Island Falls School System before moving to Pennsylvania; Cornelius, Benjamin, and Joseph all settled around Pleasant Pond and were very active in the area's development.

The aftermath of the Civil War played an important role in the development of Island Falls, Maine, and the homesteading of the area around Pleasant Pond. During the war, with many of the town's men off fighting, the town found itself to be battling the ravages of diphtheria as it raged throughout the area, with many families losing all their children. Countless young adults, those too young to fight or who had chosen to stay home to work while attempting to hold their families together, also succumbed to the dreaded disease. For some unknown reason, children and young adults found themselves the most susceptible to this disease. Following the war, although the town was weakened by despair and suffering from their great losses, the townspeople opened their hearts and arms to the returning veterans and all new homesteaders.

Accelerating Pleasant Pond's prosperity and growth was the return of three greatly decorated Civil War veterans who began projects on the pond: Cornelius Lane, finishing the Lane Homestead; Benjamin Walker, developing the Walker Settlement (now Va-Jo-Wa Golf Course); Joseph W. Edwards, starting Birch Point Campground and Cottages.

▼ *Family picnic on Pleasant Pond, about 1900 (Courtesy of Island Falls Historical Society)*

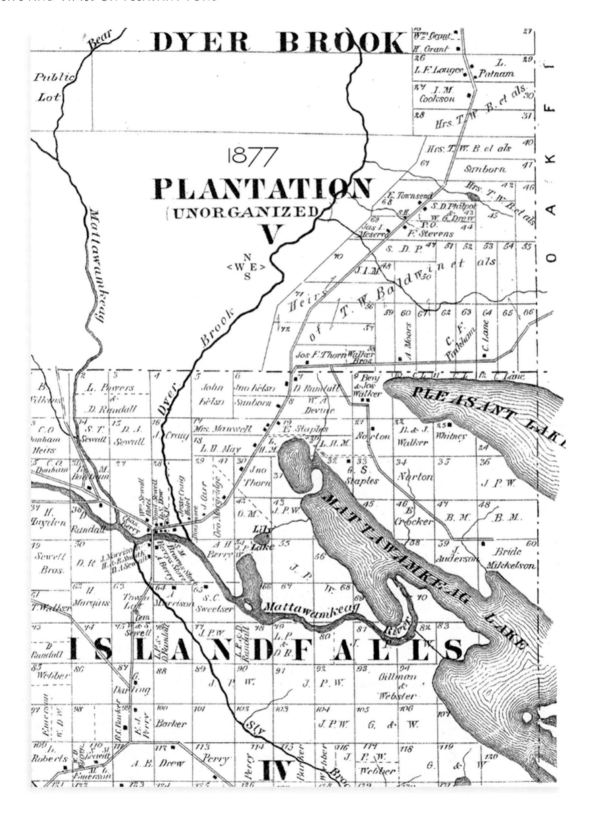

Charles G. Norton and family, about 1860 (Courtesy of Island Falls Historical Society)

THE WALKER SETTLEMENT AND VA-JO-WA GOLF COURSE

Francis Dinsmore, the original settler of Lots 21 and 34, the Walker Upper Farm, met the Kellogg brothers, John W. and Charles F., about 1860, when they moved from Gorham, Maine. Discovering Pleasant Pond, John W. purchased Lot 9, now hole #6 and #7 of Va-Jo-Wa Golf Course (named after Vaughan Walker and his sons, John and Warren) from co-owners G. W. Nickerson and Francis Dinsmore. Charles F. Kellogg purchased Lots 21, 22, and 10.

Kellogg Spring House (Photo by Sandra Newman)

The Kellogg Spring is located on Lot 10. According to Alexis Glidden, the spring is so pure "campers living nearby still hike here for drinking water." If you go for water, you will see the remains of the original spring house and the foundation where food was kept during the summer months, before refrigeration.

A small one-room schoolhouse was built around 1890 on Lot 10, near the bend in the pond known as the Kellogg Place. The schoolhouse was later moved to its present location. The original schoolhouse is the little yellow place next to Birch Point Lodge, the Tingley Cottage.

*Tingley Cottage
(Photo by Sandra
Newman)*

Charles F. Kellogg left shortly after purchasing his land, but not before selling Lot 21 to Benjamin Walker's brother-in-law, George Norton. George and his wife, Abby, had moved up from Searsport, Maine, in 1873 to manage the Barker Ridge Farm.

John W. Kellogg sold his property and a small cabin to Benjamin R. Walker, (Vaughan Walker's grandfather) and his brother, Joseph C., when they too moved up from Searsport, Maine, in 1873. Sally (Walker) Cyr and Mary (Hathaway) Sherwood remember playing in the old run-down cabin—the cabin that was on hole #4 of Va-Jo-Wa Golf Course.

Vaughan Walker and his wife, Doris, raised their three sons, Vaughan Jr. (Charlie), John, and Warren, and three daughters, Annette, Connie, and Sally on the Walker Settlement—the farm noted for raising registered Holstein cows. When the Walker's family farm was all but destroyed by fire in the summer of 1965, Vaughan followed his sports' passion and built the Va-Jo-Wa Golf Course. Today golfers find the old farm-turned-golf-course quite challenging with its steep hills, numerous sand traps, and more cow ponds than need be! According to Sally (Walker) Cyr, "Cows were the last to step on the golf course before golfers!"

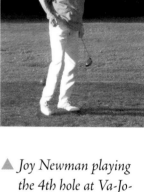

6th hole at Va-Jo-Wa Golf Course (Photo by Sandra Newman)

I remember playing with Mom: we were playing the front 9, and she teased me, "Sandy, you would be good if you practiced, concentrated, took the game seriously, and played more." Oh, I agreed.

I still keep three balls in each pocket just to be sure because I get tired of looking for the lost ones! The course is one where you start out with one ball and just might end up with six!

Joy Newman playing the 4th hole at Va-Jo-Wa Golf Course (Photo by Sandra Newman)

Vaughan Walker meeting First Lady Eleanor Roosevelt while she was staying at the Ellis Farm in Dyer Brook, Maine (Courtesy of Walker Family)

▲ Dr. Newman with Francis Cyr's
workhorse team on Pond Road
(Courtesy of Sally Cyr)

▲ Ferd Walker and friend
with workhorse team,
Walker Settlement
(Courtesy of Walker
Family)

SEPTEMBER 14, 1911—
*An old-fashioned paring bee was
held at the home of Mr. and Mrs.
George Walker (now Vaughan
Walker's) at Pleasant Pond on
Tuesday. A large number were in
attendance and greatly enjoyed
the occasion. About 4 barrels of
apples were pared and strung,
after which substantial refresh-
ments were served and a social
hour enjoyed.*

—SAMUEL R. CRABTREE
News Items

The Walker Family, 1920 (Courtesy of Walker Family)

WHITNEY POINT

Lot 23, Whitney Point, was purchased by Charles Whitney in 1879, and he lived there (until about 1900 when he sold to John Lane) with his brother, George, his wife, Susan, and their children: four daughters, Theodoria, Mattie, Minerva, and Ella, and their son, Emulus. If you go to Whitney Point, you might be able to see the foundation of the house they built while clearing the land for planting apple trees. It was after they left that the Edwards swam their cattle across the pond to pasture in these open fields, a distance of a half mile.

Whitney Point (Photo by Sandra Newman)

THE SCHOOLS AND "THE COUNTY"

▲ *The Barker Ridge School (Courtesy of Island Falls Historical Society)*

Aroostook County is Maine's northernmost county and New England's largest county, and is known for its hilly terrain and countless streams and lakes. The county was formed in March, 1839. Bordered by Canada—Québec to the west and northwest, and New Brunswick to the north and east— Aroostook's northern boundary is defined by the St. Francis and the St. John rivers. The county's residents proudly admit to being from "The County," whose name, Aroostook, is derived from a Native American word meaning "beautiful river." Pleasant Pond is located in Aroostook's southern region, an area settled mostly by English and Irish immigrants who learned of the area's rich, fertile fields made up of soil called Caribou loam.

In 1828, Congress made provision for a military road, completed in 1832 by the U.S. Army, that would connect the Bangor Military Post to Houlton Military Post, on the Canadian border. The excellent highway also opened up the beautiful, undiscovered regions in northern Maine. Alfred Moore, his two brothers, Alvah and Charles, and five children joined the pioneers who took advantage and moved from Gouldsboro, Maine, in 1859. Together the brothers purchased Lot 37 in Island Falls, now Ralph Porter's Farm. Alfred later purchased Lot 60 in Dyer Brook and cleared all but 24 acres before being drafted into the Civil War. After returning from the war, The Honorable Mr. Wiggins claimed Alfred lived on the farm for only a short time before selling to Mr. Albert Kelso, who later sold to Joseph W. Edwards in 1879.

It was while living on the now Edwards Farm that the Moore children attended the Walker-Edwards-Lane School along with the Walker, Edwards, and Lane children.

During the late 1800s and the early 1900s, with more pioneers moving into Island Falls and the surrounding areas, districts starting building their own one-room schoolhouses. These buildings, with their open-floor concept, were particularly suited for community life and often served as churches, polling places, courtrooms, meeting halls and frequently, gathering places for social events. These small schools were located within walking distance of the students' homes, anywhere from ½ mile to 2 miles one way. Schools with an added portico were more treasured as they helped to eliminate the icy, cold blasts of air felt when the door was opened. When there was no need for them on the family farm, the students attended school anywhere from 45 to 60 days, studying spelling and the three Rs.

▲ *The Old Log School (Courtesy of Island Falls Historical Society)*

Prior to September 6, 1858, when Island Falls became an organized plantation, Island Falls and the surrounding areas were considered unorganized plantations, and the pioneer children were educated through subscription. Subscription meant a school was funded by monthly tuition fees paid to the teacher by the parents. From the tuition, the teacher was responsible for finding a place for the students to study, paying the building's rent, and finding a place to room and board.

Once an organized plantation, the Island Falls subscription schools became district schools. District 1 was the Old Log School, built in 1859, where the Island Falls Grammar School was located, now the Island Falls Municipal Building. The Barker Ridge School, built in 1863, became District 2. The Hornby School, built near the head of Mattawamkeag Lake in 1873, became District 3. The Walker-Edwards-Lane School, built around 1885, became District 4.

▼ *The Walker-Edwards-Lane School (Courtesy of Island Falls Historical Society)*

THE TREES

"April 30, the ice went out of Pleasant Pond on April 24, the earliest it has been known to go out for the past forty-three years."
—SAMUEL R. CRABTREE
News Items

▼ *Lower end of Pleasant Pond at the outlet for the East Branch of Mattawamkeag River (Photo by Sandra Newman)*

Around 1875, spruce, fir, and pine trees were being harvested around the pond, and for this purpose, a dam was built at the outlet. Log drivers drove logs down the pond, out the outlet to the East Branch of the Mattawamkeag River, then down the Mattawamkeag River to the Penobscot River in Bangor, Maine. Joe Edwards claims, "One can still see where the earth was removed and used in the dam." There was also a saw mill on the pond at one time, in the upper cove near Birch Point, but it lasted only a few years. With all the hemlock trees in the area during the later-1800s and early-1900s, The Island Falls Proctor & Hunt Company became the largest tannery in New England, processing 1,600 sides of leather per day.

CHAPTER 2

The Powers Camp and Trust

Born in Essex, England, in 1639, Walter Powers came to America at the age of 14. It is believed he and the Sheppard family were first acquainted in Essex, and he was indentured to Deacon Ralph and Thankes (Thankeslord) Sheppard when he sailed to America with them. They landed at Salem, Massachusetts, in 1654. His indenture lasted six years until 1660. Apparently, Walter and the Deacon's daughter, Trial, could not wait for the formalities of marriage, and they were caught in *flagrante delicto*, an act extremely frowned at the time. Practicing the Puritan Code of Ethics, the Elders of Concord, Massachusetts, wanted them flogged, but because of the Deacon's position in the church they were married rather quickly. Betrothed in Malden, Massachusetts, January 11, 1660, Walter and Trial Sheppard later had seven sons and two daughters.

▲ *Governor Llewellyn Powers (Courtesy of the Powers Family)*

Walter and Trial settled in or near Concord in what was called Concord Village, now Littleton, Massachusetts. Mary Powers, daughter of Walter and brother of Daniel, may have been the Mary referred to in an account of the killing of two brothers, Jacob and Isaac Sheppard, as they were threshing in their barn in Concord Village. In the account, Mary was said to be their "sister" but might have been their niece as there is no record of them having a sister and the child Mary, about 15 years old at the time, was the same age as Mary Powers.

Mary, according to the account, had been looking out for Indians against a feared surprise attack when they surprised her and took her captive and then proceeded to the barn and killed her "brothers." Later Mary made a heroic escaped from the Indians encampment, stealing away while her captors slumbered and taking a horse they had stolen from Lancaster and a saddle from under the head of one of the sleeping Indians. What happened to Mary while she was with the Indians is not recorded. She later married Lieutenant Joseph Wheeler. She is not a direct ancestor of any of the current members of the Powers clan.

—AVERILL POWERS

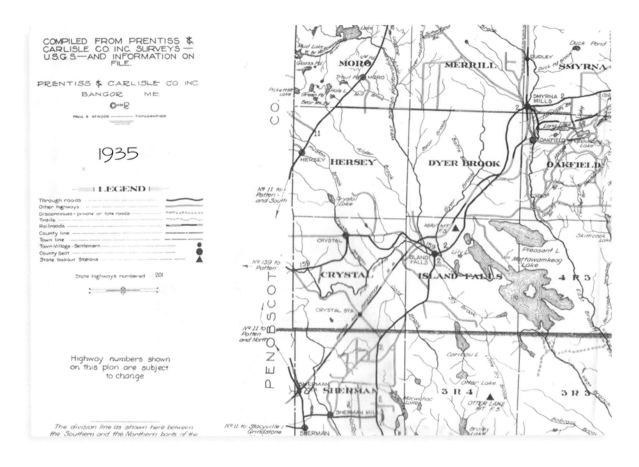

Seems Ol' Walter was quite the cagey entrepreneur. He was able to build himself quite substantial landholdings in the towns of Littleton and Nashoba, Massachusetts, acquiring a third of the town of Nashoba directly from the Indians. These towns were adjacent at the time, and they have since been incorporated into Littleton. In a fit of true Puritan frugality, the old Powers graveyard was dismantled and plowed over at some date, and the headstones were used to build a stone wall. Walter's headstone was later unearthed and is now on display in the Littleton Historical Society.

AVERILL explained the family lineage: *Father was Philip Llewellyn Powers, whose father was Walter A. Powers, whose father was Llewellyn Powers, (Governor of Maine), whose father was Arba Powers, whose father was Phillip Powers, whose father was Levi Powers, whose father was Peter Powers, whose father was Daniel Powers, son of Walter. Records of Walter come from Middlesex County (1654) and Concord Village (1660).*

Governor Llewellyn Powers was born in Pittsfield, Maine, on October 14, 1836. After attending Colby College, Waterville, Maine, he received his law degree from Union University, Albany, New York, in 1860. He moved to Houlton, Maine, in 1861, where he commenced practicing law. During his illustrious and notable career, Powers was the Prosecuting Attorney for Aroostook County from 1864 to 1871, and Collector of Customs for the District of Aroostook from 1868 until 1872, serving six terms in the Maine House of Representatives, his last term as the Speaker (1895). He was elected Governor of Maine (1897–1901), and numerous times elected into the Maine Republican Congress, where he served until his death, July 28, 1908.

Llewellyn was the politician who had inherited his family predilection for real estate. In 1896, he acquired the northern half of Township 4 Range 3 in Aroostook County, Maine: this included two-thirds of Pleasant Pond and most of Skitacook Lake. His appreciation of Aroostook County's wild lands led him to purchase a total of 175,000 acres of timberland all over the State of Maine, even crossing into New Brunswick, Canada. Some of this land he later donated to the Bangor and Aroostook Railroad as rights of way and subscribed $6,000 toward the construction of the Houlton Road.

Governor Powers was a statesman. At the time of his death, he was remembered in glowing terms by many U.S. Senators, Congressmen, and many respected dignitaries. The accolades at his funeral were very respectable and full of praise, and the eulogies were memorable, but no mention was made of his very colorful character or his life's several illustrious moments, including the Powers/Carey Trial. Seems Llewellyn was accused of "having his way" with an African-American servant in a snow bank. He did win the libel suit, but the transcript provides a colorful insight into the life and times of Llewellyn and northern Maine in general.

Mr. Powers purchased all this land for approximately 10¢ or 15¢ an acre, and kept the land until 1940 or 1945, and then his son Walter sold it for approximately $10 or $15 an acre, and Joe claimed he wished he had kept it all. He sold it all; I take it back, he sold all but about 10,000 acres, right down to the foot of Pleasant Pond.

—JOE EDWARDS

When he was running for re-election to one of his positions, he was campaigning in a Bangor & Aroostook railroad car, pressing the flesh up and down the aisle. Lore has it one old salt said to another, "There's Llew Powers, they say he's part Indian." The other replied, "The Indians don't." This is presumably a reference to the earlier mentioned Powers/Sheppard girl who was abducted by the Nashoba Indians, but is probably not true since the girl in question was not a direct ancestor.

—PHILIP POWERS

Powers Hunting Camp (Courtesy of the Island Falls Historical Society)

Walter Powers, Governor Llewellyn Powers' son, was a captain in the Marines during World War I and fought at the front in the trenches. According to his grandsons, "It was said he would lead his troops into battle so that he wouldn't be picked off as an officer, but some say he did so because he knew his troops wouldn't shoot him in the back." It was after the war, in 1917, when Walter returned to his family's secluded spot on the lower end of Pleasant Pond and began building the old hunting camp. What started out as a simple hunting camp with a basic kitchen and heated by a massive fireplace built with sand hauled from Sand Cove on a scow, today looks like an upside down ship. Walter's grandson, Philip A., jokingly commented, "If you were to upend the cottage it would probably float down the Pleasant Pond."

Frank Bell was the Bath, Maine, shipwright Walter hired to design the camp. Supposedly standing only 4-foot 2-inches tall in his stocking feet, this imaginative builder created the tightly designed "old hunting camp." It is a marvel of intricate woodwork, with rooms so small one has to duck down entering the many tiny rooms, and the Powers are so tall! There is a bell tower, built in footlockers under bed frames, cubbyholes under narrow stairways, twisting passageways, and balconies with moveable railings that interchange. Imagine lifting a railing and using it for a ladder, or having the door you just opened become a table top. The cottage, built in pieces, is such a fun puzzle with its many secret panels and passageways. Philip's father often said it was full of architectural follies. For everyone to enjoy staying in this delightful treasure, the sons share

Powers' original Old Town canoe, built 1924 (Photo by Sandra Newman)

in "staying rights." The Grange Hall, built about the same time, was first used as the tool shed. In the 1930s, a second floor was added for the boys' bunkroom.

Walter Powers loved to travel abroad and often brought back imaginative architectural ideas for his cottage. After one trip to Russia, he came back with the great idea of constructing an onion dome on the top of the main section of the cabin, but the Maine harsh winters put a damper on this wild idea. They did have a water tower on the top at one time. A 200- to 300-foot hose was placed in the outlet, and a ram pumped water to the water tower. It is claimed you could always hear the ram going when someone was using the water.

Walter Powers had five children: Philip, Peter, Denise, Naomi, and Neville. They each had children, and it is a family of boys. Of the fifteen grandchildren and six great-grandchildren there are only seven girls. Because more space was needed, a second home was started in 1993. It took seven years to build the new house. With no road, all the supplies had to be brought down from Birch Point over the ice using either a snow groomer or sled in the winter. The great house is a Katahdin Forest Product kit assembled by Craig Kennedy and Joey Edwards. Craig and Joey built the magnificent 40-foot fireplace from rocks Craig collected from the nearby lakes.

Later, in the 1940s, Walter and my Uncle Neville would come down the pond in our 1920s-era Old Town canvas canoe mounted with a small outboard motor and heavily laden with all their clothing and supplies. We all know how the west wind can pick up quite a fuss, and so they must have been a sight to see, bouncing along in the canoe 5 miles down the pond.

—PHILIP POWERS

▲ *Back: Averill,*
Philip, Peter,
Joe Edwards,
Kristopher; Front:
Alexander, Nikolas
(Courtesy of the
Edwards Family)

Philip, Averill, and Alexander were more than happy to share stories with me about George Dow, who was like an uncle to them. From him, they learned how to fish the pond, appreciate the wildlife they lived amongst, and the beauty and serenity of the surrounding woods. Philip A. remembers him as "a combination wizard, grandfather figure, and saint who knew every rock and cranny of the pond and the land around it."

The family has wonderful memories of their father's friendship with Joe Edwards and Stewart White, remembering how the three waged many of the day's battles, including the Town of Island Falls attempting to annex T4 R3. Philip, Joe, and Stewart worked tirelessly on this battle, involving politicians including the dynamic state Senator Margaret Ludwig. The annexation was ultimately defeated in Augusta, but not without a considerable amount of heartfelt haggling.

They have fun stories of the good-hearted character, Emile Robichaud. Among the Powers' and many other pond residents' cherished possessions is ownership of one of the 150 fishing creels Emile Robichaud handcrafted with pride and gave as gifts.

▲ *Emile Robichaud's*
fishing creel

They also remember Nels Martin, a friend of their grandfather's in the 1930s and '40s who lived in the hunting camp directly across the pond from the Powers. Even though Nels lived off the land and was known to be an exceptional hunter and trapper, he was the dealer for International Farm Equipment. Joe told me Nels had the first and only houseboat on the pond and "it was a fair-sized houseboat that Nels lived on for a number of years."

It was while governor that Mr. Powers joined forces with President Theodore Roosevelt and other political leaders passionate about Island Falls, Mattawamkeag Lake, Pleasant Pond and the surrounding area. Together they sought ways for all the timberland to be in harmony with growth. Philip A., Governor Powers' great-grandson, is an environmental advocate. When his father, Philip L., passed away in 1993, he took over management of the Trust: the 11,000 acres of pristine woodland within T4 R3. This Trust encompasses the lower end of the pond: from Sand Cove, all the way around to Barker Rocks, and Skitacook and Mud lakes. Within the borders of the Trust lie deer-winterizing habitats, a healthy black bear population, eagle nesting grounds, and over a million trees.

Today, forestry management plays an important part in the Powers' protection of the fragile ecosystem of the land they inherited. Philip L. introduced the concept of sustainable forestry in the 1960s, which was considered quite eccentric. At the time, lumbermen generally clear cut, moving from one parcel to the next. Later, when good timber stands became scarce, Powers ideas proved right. With selective harvesting and intelligent forest management the rule, not the exception, for their property's mixed stand of timber. They have developed and refined the science with the help of Ted Shina and Peter Triandefillou who have been with them as their timber managers for over thirty years, since before 1980. The result: the Powers' stands are far superior in quality to most in the state; they get 22 cords an acre rather than nature's normal 18 cords. The Powers trustees intend to keep it undeveloped, forever.

Right to left: Hiram, Peter, Alexander, Philip, Averill, and Llewellyn Powers (Courtesy of the Powers Family)

The family members are also active supporters of efforts to maintain and improve the pond's exceptional water quality. Philip informed me that our natural spring-fed pond is a very delicate water supply, turning over only once every seven years, and is much improved from when prior generations dumped their trash in the middle and septic systems drained into the pond. Let's keep protecting what we all have grown to love and enjoy.

Philip A., brothers, Averill and Alexander, their uncle Neville, and cousins, Peter, Hiram, and Llewellyn, have recently become trustees of the trust, and they will jointly bear in the responsibility of managing and preserving the property for future generations. It is their intention to make the decisions necessary to preserve the pond, Skitacook, and the surrounding lands for their descendants and for those who love and appreciate the beauty of nature. We are fortunate to live on a pond that is protected by a governor who had a love for the land and a sense of family tradition—two traits often associated with the people of Maine.

▶ *Two loons (Photo by Sandra Newman)*

CHAPTER 3

The Edwards Homestead

Edwards Homestead with Birch Point cottages and original dining hall in background; oat fields in foreground with stacks of oats; Walker Settlement is to the right, 1934 (Courtesy of Island Falls Historical Society)

OPPORTUNITY KNOCKS OFTENTIMES IN THE MOST UNSUSPECTING PLACES

Little did William Joseph Edwards suspect when he moved his family from Searsport, Maine, and purchased the Alfred Moore Farm in 1879, he was beginning five generations of the Edwards Family being part of Maine tourism.

▶ *Birch Point church picnic (Courtesy of Island Falls Historical Society)*

AUGUST 30, 1906—
The Congregational Sunday School held its annual picnic at Edwards Point, Pleasant Pond, on August 21, the free Baptist held theirs on August 23. Dexter Smart of Oakfield, with his gasoline launch, was employed by each school to give free rides for the children.

—SAMUEL R. CRABTREE

News Items

Ralph Edwards explains in his *History of Pleasant Lake* that his father, W. F. Edwards, took over the farm when Ralph's Uncle Dan passed away in 1912. His uncle had inherited the family farm when his father, Joseph W. Edwards, passed away about 1900 and his mother, Genevre, married Benjamin Walker. W. F. and his wife, Melvina, lived on the farm until 1921 when they moved to Island Falls so the boys could attend the Old Log School. Joe Edwards recalls, "Father worked in George York's potato house, and the boys attended school. Like today's pond people, we would spend the long, cold, dreary winters in Island Falls and move to the pond in early May to spend the glorious summer months on the farm. We did this for many years, long after the Walker-Edwards-Lane School had closed due to low enrollment. From where we lived in town, Shep, Lawrence, Danny, and Ralph drove a horse and sleigh to the school in the winter. Mom always worried about them getting back after dark, as the boys would be freezing!"

▶ *Dan Edwards, Scott Adams, and W. F. Edwards, 1934 (Courtesy of the Edwards Family)*

It was actually Melvina Edwards who had the idea that tourism was the way of the future and urged her husband to build the log cabins about 1924. The first cabin they built was Cabin #4, and another one was built every summer after that through the 1930s and '40s.

W. F. continued in the potato brokering business and joyfully managed the Dance Pavilion he had acquired due to no fault of his own. Melvina, also very enterprising, started her own restaurant in the first lodge they built in 1928.

When you take on projects like this, everyone needs a special friend, and they found theirs in Scott Adams. Scott was the area Fire Warden around 1928. He enjoyed canoeing 5 miles down Pleasant Pond and walking 20 miles into the woods, checking on fires the fisherman may have started. Scott may have been a great hunter and fisherman, but he was a dreadfully lonely man. It was this extreme loneliness that had him visiting the various overnight camps on the pond when he returned from the woods. Visiting the camps, he would exchange brook trout for conversation, and one of his stops just happened to be with Melvina Edwards.

After a while, with an abundance of fish and not a clue of what to do with it all, Melvina started serving breakfasts of trout to the guests staying in the overnight camps built by her husband and sons. This was the beginning of *Birch Point Cottages, with Breakfast.* With Scott Adams providing the trout for the breakfasts, Melvina frying it up, Joe and his brothers providing accommodations, everyone was happy. "Scott gained much-desired friendships, the tourist staying in the cottages got fed, and the excess trout got eaten. What more could we ask?"

▲ *Original Cabin #4 (Courtesy of the Edwards Family)*

▼ *The original restaurant, built in 1928, with lunch room added in 1931; dismantled in 1955 (Courtesy of the Edwards Family)*

▶ *Birch Point Pavilion, about 1924. Fogg's Famous Dance Band, Brockton, Massachusetts, with W. F. Edwards on porch (Courtesy of the Island Falls Historical Society)*

▼ *Pavilion at Pleasant Lake Farm before renamed Birch Point Campground and Cottages (Courtesy of the Island Falls Historical Society)*

recalls Joe. "In the beginning everyone worked: Mom was cooking, Julia was waitressing, the boys were building. We all did our share, and more."

DANCE PAVILION

Dancing was the craze of the Roaring '20s, and the perfect time for a dance pavilion. As luck would have it, in the enjoyable spring of 1922, Harold Hall had arrived on the scene with the idea of a dance pavilion on Pleasant Pond. Discovering Birch Point, Harold signed a lease with W. F. Edwards, agreeing to pay $150 a year, for three years, for the location. Pavilion construction was completed early August 1922 and the first dance, August 12, 1922, was a raving success attracting 125 decked out couples from all around the area. They arrived driving their new touring cars. They arrived after bouncing along the roads in their horse and buggy, or they paddled up from the lower end of the pond in their Old Town canoe. They didn't care how they arrived, they were going dancing!

And I hear it was a rowdy, totally entertaining, dancing celebration!

Unfortunately, Mr. Hall did not pay for the lumber he had purchased from Northern Woodenware or for the lease of the land at the end of three years. This oversight allowed W. F. Edwards to take over the Dance Pavilion. By paying Northern Woodenware for the lumber Mr. Hall had purchased, W. F. was able to keep the pavilion open. Ask many people in the area, they will tell you that the pavilion became a major area attraction. This was also when Birch Point got its name. The dancers and campers kept calling it Birch Point after the magnificent white birch trees that surrounded the area.

Dot (Longstaff) Ericson remembered the Pavilion romantically; it is where she met her husband, Winn Ericson. The story goes: Winn was a drummer in the Melody Boys Band. Smitten as he was, he asked her out—Dot's first date alone in a car with a man. On the way home, he leaned over to give her a kiss just as the Bradford Mill on Fish Stream exploded. Thinking it was her home, the Longstaff Farm, she instantly made Winn take her home. Yes, they were married and lived happily ever after.

▲ *Birch Point Pavilion waterfront (Courtesy of the Island Falls Historical Society)*

CLARA HATHAWAY, "Oh, I remember the Pavilion! We danced, and danced. Oh, we had such fun! The boys from Houlton would come down, and we danced with them. We never knew their names; we didn't care. We just danced the night away. Oh, it was fun."

STELLA LARLEE danced many nights away at the Pavilion while working at Camp Roosevelt, along with many people in the area. Just mention the Dance Pavilion and you will hear, "Oh, how I remember the Dance Pavilion. What a wonderful, gay, fun time we all had dancing nights away!"

THE POWERS CLAN, Phil, Peter, Nonnie, Nevil, and Denise, all piled into the red Old Town canoe, and paddled up the pond happy to dance the night away many times at the Dance Pavilion.

JOE'S STORY ACCORDING TO JOE

The opportunity knocked for Joe Edwards in 1946 when he inherited the family farm from his father and mother, W. F. and Melvina Edwards. As luck would also have it, the previous year his brother, Lawrence, had plowed 8 of the 175 acres before he moved to the coast of Maine. With no idea as to why not, Joe decided to try potato farming. "I furnished the seed and fertilizer for Garfield Slauenwhite, who I hired to plant, harvest, and put the potatoes in the potato house. It was after all the hard work, did we discover all the potatoes were full of wire worms and they couldn't be eaten, sold, or used."

Once Joe and Garfield realized the potatoes couldn't be sold on the open market, they were desperate. They needed an answer as to what to do with all those potatoes. Any solution was better than dumping the crop. Searching around, Joe discovered a plant in Philadelphia, Pennsylvania, backed by a government program, attempting to grind potatoes into alcohol. "I had discovered a way to get rid of those wire-worm-filled potatoes. I loaded my potatoes into a freight car and shipped them off to Philadelphia. After a good while, I received a check from the U.S. government for $2,000. I had shipped 500 barrels, and I received $4 a barrel. That was barely enough to cover the cost of seed, fertilizer, planting, harvesting, shipping, and handing over to Garfield Slauenwhite, the agreed upon, half the proceeds!" With these earth-shattering results, Joe decided to go out of the potato business. Imagine!

▲ *W. F. and Melvina Edwards, Ma and Pa, 1934 (Courtesy Edwards Family)*

Rustic Birch Point Cabins, 1934 (Courtesy of the Edwards Family)

Joe admitted to me he had learned his lesson. "I was not a farmer, but I still needed to make a living. Having the Dance Pavilion and the cabins, they were my salvation. My father had acquired the pavilion from Harold Hall in 1924, who had originally built the pavilion in 1922, on land he leased from my father, and when Mr. Hall could no longer meet expenses, he had to sell, you see. Now with Cabin #4 my brothers Ralph, Danny, and Keith had help built in 1926, and with the idea that there was a future in recreation, Birch Point Campgrounds was started."

Joe remembers, "In the beginning the original cabins were very raw: no plumbing, no electric, and no screens." He claims it was amazing people came, and proudly remembers, "In 1929, my father and cousin, George Dow, went to the Oxbow to look at some log cabins to get an idea of how to construct them. The first cabin was built that summer, and it was quite a building, Cabin #4: 24 foot x 16 foot, and still used today." After the first cabin, Joe and his brothers, Daniel and Keith, along with Scott Adams, cut logs and built one every summer for the next six years. In 1946, they built cottages with upgrades: water, roads, electric, and sewage.

Inside original cabin (Courtesy of the Edwards Family)

▶ *Scott Adams, Fred Sewell, and Bill Sewall (on truck) hauling the lumber (Courtesy of the Edwards Family)*

▲ *Herb Hanson moving logs up pond, 1956 (Courtesy of the Edwards Family)*

"We even had postcards printed by Barbara Kennison, John Kennison's daughter, along with a brochure for advertising."

Then disaster struck in 1955—excess snow caused the Dance Pavilion to cave in. Joe remembers, "The Dance Pavilion was located where the campground is now. With people still coming to stay in the cottages who needed a restaurant and a place for outdoor water activities, it was decided not to rebuild the Dance Pavilion because we thought the idea of dancing might not be as lucrative as a campground, lodge, and restaurant serving meals to vacationers."

Along with these speculative ideas, using plans drawn up by a Boston architect, Joe built the 100 foot x 40 foot new lodge in 1956. With the help of Scott Adams, Herb Hanson, Bill and Fred Sewall, and George Dow, Joe cut 100,000 feet of lumber for the project: "I cut 50,000 feet on the farm, and the additional 50,000 feet on Powers' land, at the foot of the pond." The second floor of the lodge, with those wonderful large windows overlooking the lake, became home to Joe, Delma, Scott, and Steven when they moved into the spacious apartment from the farmhouse.

From around 1958 to about 1965, Red Cross swimming lessons were

Birch Point swimming area with float where Red Cross swimming lessons were offered, 1945–1965 (Courtesy of the Edwards Family)

Swimming area in the foreground; the Pleasant Pond Lumber Mill, built and operated 1940–1945, cut lumber all around the shore and up to several feet of the hillsides (Courtesy of the Island Falls Historical Society)

offered every summer with Lib Harmon, Pat Emerson, Charlie Walker, Larry and Anne Thompkins, Reneva (Jones) Smith, Phil Faulkner, Ed Quinlan, Sally (Walker) Cyr, Sandy Newman, and Mike Corveau among the swimming instructors. Swimmers came to the Point from all around the pond, and the towns of Island Falls, Smyrna, Oakfield, and Crystal, but sadly they only lasted a few years. There was a float at one time, the gathering place for all the "pond kids," but without a lifeguard on duty, if anything happened, Joe was responsible, so the float was taken out. As it was, with the campground becoming more popular with campers, the area available for lessons became too busy, so Birch Point Swimming Area sadly was closed to the public in 1965.

In 1960, bowling became one of the lodge's highlights. With everyone thinking he was nuts, Joe traveled to the McToKa Club in Caribou, Maine, with $400 dollars in his pocket and purchased a 6-lane candlepin bowling alley. After bringing the bowling alley back to the lodge, he installed it in the lower level. This new enterprise grew to the point that he was making $1,000 to $1,500 a week on

Original bowling alley (Courtesy of the Edwards Family)

an idea people thought crazy. For two or three years in a row, the Maine Public Service held their bowling tournament in the bowling alley and their banquet in the 100-seat dining room. At one time, forty bowling teams were registered, playing 4 days a week with five people per team. Today, there are 15 teams. Play goes from October through May with bowlers coming from Sherman, Patten, Oakfield, Island Falls, and points in between.

Next Joe tried skiing. Using a tractor, a rope, and Birch Point Hill, Joe introduced skiing to Island Falls. I can remember very well breaking a ski and getting a great pair of black Northland skis at the Island Falls Hardware Company, owned by Wilson Palmer. Scott Edwards had it worse; he broke a leg. Anyone remember après-ski at the Edwards and having oyster stew?

In 1965, oil heating and cement foundations were added to cot-

Interior of original cabins before oil heat and insulation, rented out May 1 through November, early hunting season. (Courtesy of the Edwards Family)

Birch Point Campground, 1965 (Courtesy of the Edwards Family)

tages, making them available for year-round rental. The National Starch Company often rented two or three cottages at a time. Today, Birch Point Campground and Cottages is a year-round recreational spot with ten cottages totally insulated and oil heated. Not so thirty-five years ago!

THE STORY GOES, BELIEVE IT OR NOT!

Our Joe Edwards, proud developer of Birch Point, on our beloved Pleasant Pond, decided about 1965 to heat the seven cabins, his home, and the laundry building with oil. At that time, heating oil was 10¢ a gallon, and knowing he had a 5,000-gallon tank and oil was cheaper than wood, guess what?

The story goes: Joe and Smokey James buried the 5,000-gallon tank beside Cabin #1. Using copper tubing, they hooked the seven cabins, lodge, and laundry up for oil heat. The new system made it through a beautiful summer, gorgeous fall, and delightful winter—then spring arrived with frost heaves!! Lo and behold, the copper tubing broke, flooding 100 feet of the pond in front of the cabin. Luckily, with ice still not out, the oil was contained in an ice blockade. Not knowing what to do, Joe asked his friendly friend Emile Robichaud standing nearby, "What the _____ am I suppose to do?" Emile replied, "Set her fire!" With this, Joe tossed a match, and he burned the oil away with no residue left.

Still today, with a roving permit to cut wood anywhere around the pond, Joe and his family are able to use the lumber to maintain the cottages and to build and rebuild picnic tables and various outbuildings. To accommodate the renters, campers, and pond people, there is a small marina supplying gas, kayaks, canoes, and boat rentals. The campground, which was started on the old Dance Pavilion site with just three or four campsites, now has sixty-five to seventy-five well-maintained sites.

▲ *Joe Edwards with*
9-pound salmon
(Courtesy of the
Edwards Family)

JOE'S FISHING STORY

See, I still call this a pond. When the natives started living in Island Falls, they were either going to "the pond" or "the lake." They didn't go to Mattawamkeag Lake or Pleasant Pond; it was just the pond or the lake for fishing and even picnicking. The pond doesn't have any inlets that amount to anything; it is a spring-fed pond, and I lived here all my life except for three years in the Army Air Force. (Between 1942 and 1945, Joe was 8th Army/Air Corps stationed in England flying thirty missions over Germany as a tail- and ball-gunner).

I have watched the highs and lows of it, and I have seen sad times in water height. I didn't put a measure on it, but it doesn't change from 2-feet high to 2-feet low from normal (65 to 70 feet), which was the height of about 2 to 4 feet in the run of a year. Generally speaking, in late-November or early-December, sometimes it will freeze all over and other times it won't freeze but part of it. I have seen it stay open until 1 or 2 days after Christmas in my time. I guess it was 1 or 2 times later than that. It stays frozen from January through April. Generally the ice leaves the pond the last days of April or the first 10 days of May, and we have a lot of pictures.

Years passed, when I started out in the early 1940s, and I put fish shacks on the ice, it produced excellent smelt fishing. I had as many as twenty shacks on the ice, and I had lights in them and had people coming out to smelt fish from Presque Isle, and as far south as Bangor and Portland, Maine. Many people from the area would come to the pond in the winter, and fish smelt. Smelts were very plentiful, as well as cusk. The fisherman would get the old cedar rails from George Walker's Cedar Fence Co. and use them for a wood fire.

It was nothing to go out there and catch; in the early morning you could get forty to fifty smelt, and up to a hundred. The limit of smelt fishing was 4 quarts, but I think now it is reduced to 2 quarts. The smelt used to run in small brooks, usually in the late April, to early May. I am told they spawn on the shores of the pond. I have never found them spawning on the shores of the pond. Back in 1984 or '85 a disease hit the smelt population and they practically disappeared. In 2007, I had a nice mess of smelt out of the pond that winter. They were approximately 5-inches long; at one time smelt averaged about 6½ to 7 inches.

In 1910, a fish screen was installed in the outlet, and the pond was stocked with some landlocked salmon. Two years later, Cornelius Lane had some small mouth bass shipped to him and he put them in the pond.

Now we put a lot of salmon in. We fish salmon in the spring and also in the deep water in the summer. And it is also heavily populated with black bass. About 1883, small mouth bass were shipped to Cornelius Lane, over on the Lane Farm, and he put them in the lake. I was told there were twenty-three bass planted in the pond amounting to tremendous bass fishing. Now in June and July it's really good bass fishing especially when the bass are spawning on the beds, and you can see large beds or nests whichever you want to call them, all over the lake. The bass will average up to 3 to 5 pounds. They are really good eating fish and taste nearly as good as a salmon, but people all want salmon today. So that's the way fish appeared. We have a few perch, and at one time pickerel. They were mainly up around the head of the pond where the water has a shallow freeze around the shoreline and it used to be quite a lot of fun.

To catch a pickerel, go to the head of the pond where there are a lot of lily pads where the pickerel hide, I was told by Dan James. Some of the edge families use to spear the pickerel: they would go up at night, spear them by putting a light on them. But pickerel now have practically disappeared.

▲ The Edwards Family: Joe and Scott (front), Steven and Joey (back) (Courtesy of the Edwards Family)

We still offer Bean-hole Beans every Saturday night, a tradition started by Father in 1925, and we'd used to serve them for the rest of the week. Sandy tells me, the best raspberry pie was made by Raymond Michaud. He used to cook in the woods and also made great molasses cookies.

—JOSEPH EDWARDS

87 years old

THE MEMORIES OF RALPH EDWARDS

The first settlement on the shore of Pleasant Lake (as it was then called) occurred in 1858 by Cornelius Lane. While working for Cyrus Barker at the Barker Ridge Farm, Cornelius came to Pleasant Lake with Francis Dinsmore, who also was working at Barker Ridge Farm. They built a raft and crossed the lake where Mr. Lane decided to settle. He came back later and

Emile Robichaud and Ralph Edwards ice fishing on Pleasant Pond, 1978 (Courtesy of the Edwards Family)

built a camp on the shore in front of the Lane Farm and settled there.

Francis Dinsmore acquired a lot where Swetts built a camp there. He cleared some land and stayed there but a couple of years.

The first reported fish in the lake were yellow perch, white perch, cusk, and trout. The trout were of two kinds—square tail and swallow tail. The swallow tail was later identified as blue black trout, which are now nearly extinct. It is believed by state biologists that only two or three lakes in the state now have any of these trout. When ice melted from the shore in the spring, the fishing was said to be pretty good for each kind of trout.

Black bass were introduced in 1878 when Mr. Stillwell was Fish and Game Commissioner. Mr. Lane went to Houlton with a wagon, got twenty-three bass, brought them back and put them in the lake. He told of stopping at every brook to give them fresh water. How they survived getting up here isn't known, but they apparently got fresh water along the way. The environment must have been perfect for them as they have multiplied and now are plentiful in both Pleasant and Mattawamkeag Lakes. Smelts were introduced in 1880, but where they came from, and who put them in seems to be lost in time.

A few lines should be written here about the mysterious disappearance of the smelts in 1984. For a couple of years, there were very few caught. In 1987, I started catching them again in the summer. The most I caught were only about 4¼-inches long, but there seemed to be plenty

◀ *Whitney Log Cabin*
(Photo by Sandra
Newman)

of them. The fish biologist hasn't an explanation of the strange disappearance except to say it happens in most lakes where there are smelts. In two or three years they return again.

The Edwards Farm was cleared in 1890, by Alfred Moore. He lived there until 1879 when my grandfather and family came from Searsport and bought it. About that time, a Mr. Kellogg acquired the lot where Bev Rand's camp is and Walker Settlement is. Soon after, Benjamin Walker, Joseph Walker, and Timothy Walker came from Searsport and acquired the Walker Settlement and Kellogg lot.

In 1879, Charles Whitney settled on the south shore of Pleasant Lake, which now is known as Whitney Point. He built a house, cleared a little land and planted quite a few apple trees. The cellar of the house is still visible, but the field and apple trees are pretty well gone by the march of time.

In 1858, when Cornelius Lane settled, he told about hearing wolves barking. He looked out on the lake and saw five or six wolves killing a deer. They took a lantern, went out and drove the wolves off, and took the deer back to their camp. He told of the wolves barking most of the night, but the wolves left the next morning. They saw no more deer until around 1880, and he never saw any more wolves.

When Llewellyn Powers was governor of Maine around 1878, he acquired the north half of T4 R3 which included about two-thirds of

*▲ Birch Point
(Photo by Sandra
Newman)*

the eastern part of Pleasant Lake. Walter Powers started building the Powers Camp in 1918. It was built by Frank Bell, retired shipwright who had come here to live with his sister, Geneva Plummer, at the Red Bridge.

The sand for the cement was brought across the lake from Sand cove on a barge. When they got a good south wind, the barge drifted across quite easily as Sand Cove was almost directly across from the Powers camp. The camp and grange building (so called) were finished in 1928.

In the late 1880s, a small lumber camp was built on the south side of Pleasant Lake Mountain below the outlet. There were quite a lot of large pine trees around the lower end of the lake which were cut, boomed over to the outlet, and driven down the outlet to the East Branch of the Mattawamkeag and on to the mills in Bangor. A dam was built in the outlet to hold water for the drive down the outlet. Just how this was built and how the dam held enough water back remains quite a mystery, which no one seems to be able to recollect. There is a large hole in the ground near the outlet from which the earth was taken to build the dam.

Sometime in the early-1900s salmon were put in the lake. A screen was put in the outlet about 1920, because it was thought the salmon were going out the outlet. The screen was removed about 1924 because Mr. Powers thought it was interfering with the pumping of water to his camp by a so-called ram. This was a 3-inch pipe that was put in the outlet for about 200 feet. When the water came out the end, a ram gadget was put on and pushed the water up to the camp through a ¾-inch pipe about 125 yards away. This gave them running water in the camp. A tank was put in the attic for water when the ram failed to work, which was quite often.

The screen was put in again about 1934, by Andrew Brittain, W. F. Edwards, D. J. Edwards, and Ralph Edwards. Salmon were being stocked quite regularly, but few were caught even though very few people fished for them. About 1918 or 1920, W. F. Edwards and George Dow got a salmon in a net that weighed 18½ pounds. An outline of this fish on sheathing paper was kept by Edwards for many years.

W. F. Edwards told of getting a much larger one in a net that got away that he says could have weighed 30 or 35 pounds. These fish, it seems quite apparent, were sea salmon that came up the rivers and stayed in the lake. This was before there were any dams on the rivers or any pollution going into the rivers. Around 1935, Dr. Frank Tarbell of Smyrna Mills got a lot of salmon fry and put them in the East Branch. For a few years after that, about all that was caught in the East Branch were small salmon 6 or 7 inches long. What salmon were caught in the lake at this time were mostly large one, 7 to 12 pounds. In the 1940s, salmon fishing was excellent in the lake, most fish weighing 3 to 4 pounds.

When I was 7 or 8 years old living on the farm, my father had a gill net which he put in the upper end of the lake in the spring. This was the first place the ice melted down to about where the electric line crossed. We pulled it every morning and generally had two or three pickerel in it. Every few mornings he would have two or three trout that would weigh 2 to 4 pounds each. In December and January of 1920–21, when the smelts were biting good, we caught a lot and shipped them to Boston along with many pounds of cusk. We got 15¢ per pound for the smelts and 12¢ per pound for the cusk. It took about twelve smelts for a pound. The freight charges were paid in Boston, so we got a few dollars and had fun catching them. It was later that a law was found on the books that forbid the selling of these fish. In those years, we were more concerned with getting something to eat than we were with the law.

It would be remiss of me if no mention were made of the early settlers in this area. The first people that came were known as settlers and where they settled was known as settlements rather than the name of the towns where they were, which probably, at that time, had not become incorporated to have a name—such as Island Falls, Oakfield, Sherman, etc.

In these early settlements where six or eight families settled, it was common for the families to get together and decide about the color pattern of some cloth to be purchased. Thus, a large bolt of cloth would be purchased for several families. Most of the men's clothes and some of the women's were made from the same bolt of cloth. When any of these people got to another town—although their names might not be known—they would be referred to as people from the Walker Settlement or the Edwards Settlement, etc., by the color of their clothes. Later on, most people had a few sheep and a spinning wheel to make yarn. I still remember my mother spinning yarn on the spinning wheel and trying to teach me, without success.

▲ *Two boys on tree (Courtesy of the Island Falls Historical Society)*

Healthwise, these early settlers had problems. One I know and tell about was what I call the "Kitchen Table Operation." When my father, W. F. Edwards, was about 17, he had a very severe lung congestion. After several months without recovering, an operation was decided upon. Dr. Boyd from Houlton or Linneus did the operation. He put father on the kitchen table at the Edwards Farm and chloroform was used as an anesthetic. Two pieces of his ribs were cut out of his left side, one about 2-inches long and the other about 1½-inches long. A tube was then put in for drainage. I still remember the pieces of ribs which were kept with the notation "pieces of ribs from Will from Dr. Boyd's operation." He recovered very nicely and lived to be 82 years old. I still recall my grandmother telling about the terrible sound as Dr. Boyd sawed the ribs off. I have sometimes wondered if the name "Old Sawbones" was first used by my grandmother.

About every area with three or four settlements had a small school for young people, although some attended school who were not so young, being 16 or 18 years old, along with the young ones. The teachers were mostly older men or women—20 years or so—who did the teaching. They generally boarded at a home in the area while teaching. Most of the schools were in session for a few weeks in the summer and early fall because of the severe winters and lack of transportation. Most of the older men went to school to learn to "cipher"—nowadays known as studying mathematics.

One of the big events that took place in this area was the "Apple Paring Bees" held at the Lane Farm every fall in September when the Duchess apples were ripe. Probably as many as forty people would come to prepare apples in different ways for the coming winter. It was held at the Lane Farm because of the many apple trees they had there—particularly Duchess.

The events I have mentioned here are what I recall of being told to me and some that I recall myself.

Around 1890, the schoolhouse from the Walker Settlement, which was located on the upper side of the road from the public landing on Pleasant Lake, was moved to a lot at Birch Point by a Mr. Crommett. When it got up by the Edwards Farmhouse, it got off the sleds, and not being able to get it back on the sleds, a lot was bought, and the schoolhouse was brought down the hill and put where it is now, and is owned by the Tingley Family.

In the early 1900s, Charles Lane, brother of John Lane, built a camp about half way between the Lane Farm and the Edwards Farm, and cleared quite a little land, 6 or 8 acres or more. When I was 6 or 7 years old, I sometimes went there for a day and helped him or tried to help burn brush for his land clearing. I remember eating with him. Once he had a can of cherries which I thought was the best thing I had ever tasted. He stayed only a few years and left. I don't have any information of where he went or what became of him.

Another clearing was made between his clearing and the Edwards Farm by some people by the name of Pinkham. Six or eight acres were cleared, but they left and never returned. These clearings were known as the "Pinkham Lots." The land on the lower side of the road was later acquired by S. C. Spratt, and the land on the upper side is now owned by Great Northern Paper Company.

Charles Edwards built a house and a barn on the west of Edwards Farm, which was later occupied by Dan James and family and later abandoned.

The Steele Camp (Photo by Sandra Newman)

The Hillman Camp was one of the earliest camps built on the lake—about 1908 or so—and is still there. (Torn down in spring of 2009, and rebuilt by Pam [Hillman] Oliver fall of 2009.) It is owned by Thomas Hillman. Some of the other older ones were Crabtree, Eldridge, Steele, and a man by the name of Statham. My brother, Dannie, and I have named him the meanest man that ever lived. He stayed here all summer, and we brought him a quart of milk daily. At the end of the week, he would give us a penny for delivering the milk.

This was not a penny a piece, but a penny for us to divide up.

About 1900, my Grandfather Edwards died. He had been in the Civil War. My grandmother later married Ben Walker, Vaughn Walker's grandfather. The farm was then taken over by my uncle, Dan Edwards.

One of my earliest memories of winter life on the farm was the preparations for winter. I recall my father going to town and bringing home about 4 barrels of flour, a barrel of sugar, 10 or 15 gallons of molasses, and about 10 pounds of crackers. There were a few years when he raised about 2 acres of wheat. After it was threshed, he went to Houlton with a wagon or sled of horses and had it milled into flour, which lasted at least a year. We had our own apples, carrots, turnips, and preserves.

Dan Edwards, my uncle, died in 1912. The farm was then taken over by my father, W. F. Edwards. I was born there in April of 1912—the first child to be born after they moved there.

About 1917, a dance pavilion was built at Birch Point by Harold Hall. My father took it over a couple of years later. It was the most popular dance spot for many miles around. When it first started, many people in the area of Island Falls, Dyer Brook, and Oakfield came by horse and buggy. Cars were just starting to get here then. Soon after, overnight camps were built and soon became quite a business.

Our early education was at Island Falls, and it was quite a problem to get to school. In the winter, we went by horse and sleigh, and in the early years, by horse and wagon in the spring and fall. After about 1920, we had a Ford Model T. Much of the time in the spring and fall we walked to school which was about 5 miles each way. We often had company as the Walker boys also were there. Sometimes in the fall when we had snow, we were the target of snowballs when we started home. My oldest brother would put the whip to the old horse to get away from the barrage of snowballs.

The Edwards Farm was situated in the extreme southern part of Dyer Brook where no other families lived with school children; a considerable controversy arose about what to do with the Edwards children because the school house in the settlement had been closed. The town of Dyer Brook decided it was too expensive to send a school team over to pick us up, and take us back to Dyer Brook. It was finally decided they would pay the tuition for the kids to go to Island Falls, but they would have to provide their own transportation. Thus it was that I started and went to school in Island Falls. I well remember my first grade. Our teacher had a reading class of twelve. If we went 12 consecutive days, we would get to the head of the class, and were rewarded with a few peanuts. I went the whole year, and never got to school 10 consecutive days. When we missed a day, we had to go to the foot of the class. Something always seemed to happen—the horse was lame, the old car wouldn't go, or it was way too cold.

Over one hundred years have passed since the first settlers settled here, but somehow much remains the same. The Walkers still have the land across the lake on the south side, the Edwards on the north, but the Lane Farm is now owned by the Quinlan Family. The Powers still own the land on the lower end on the lake.

I sometimes criticized our education department that there isn't enough taught in our schools about the early settlers in our state. We somehow are losing our early heritage about how the state was settled, land cleared, how people made a living, and progressed to where it is today. Although this may not be of much importance to many people, it does bring some thoughts of how things happened in the earlier years in this area.

—RALPH R. EDWARDS

▼ *View from Red Bridge, South Road to Linneus Corner, East Branch of Mattawamkeag River (Photo by Sandra Newman)*

After much thought, I have decided to add a post script to my history of the lake.

Before 1900, the only road to Houlton was by Pleasant Lake to the "Red Bridge" and out the South Road to Linneus Corner. I want to share a story that was told concerning the taking of the census before 1900 when the South Road was quite heavily settled. When the census was taken, the government in Washington decided they would send a man up here because they doubted anyone up here in the woods could count heads.

They sent a man from Washington. As he was going out the South Road taking the census at each house, he came to Crow Hill where a family by the name of Crow lived. The

census man made himself known. After asking their names, he said he wanted the names of their children and their ages. Mrs. Crow said there were John and James, twins age 8; also, Robin and Roberta, twins age 5; and Joseph and Jean, twins age 3.

After he had written down this information, the census taker said this was quite unusual and said, "Did you always get twins?" Mrs. Crow quickly answered, "God gracious, no, there were lots of times when we never even got one."

THE MEMORIES OF KEITH EDWARDS

In the spring of 1922, Harold Hall leased the Birch Point from William Edwards and constructed a dance pavilion, dancing being very much in vogue right after World War I. The first dance was August 1922, [attended by] 125 couples. He was to get $150 a year for the lease at the end. Hall did not pay for the lease or lumber, so William Edwards took it over and paid Northern Woodware for the lumber that Mr. Hall had bought from them but had not settled.

About 1926, my father, at the urging of my mother, built five overnight camps, which were just becoming popular. The pavilion caved in from too much snow in 1955. The first cottage on the pond was in 1903 the Crabtree camp; the next year, 1904, Harold Hillman built the camp that his son Thomas still owns. In 1860, William Walker, the Civil War veteran, came from Searsport and bought lots and settled on the present day Walker Settlement and golf course. Cornelius Lane came from Searsport and settled the Lane Farm in 1850. All three of these men—Walker, Lane, and Edwards—enlisted in the army and served in the Civil War. Mr. Edwards, being a member of the 19th Maine regiment was at Gettysburg and served at the high-water mark of the Confederacy at Cemetery Ridge during Pickett's Charge.

In 1919, Walter Powers came

Birch Point Camps, 1935 (Courtesy of the Edwards Family)

back from World War I and started construction of the Powers camp at the outlet of Pleasant Pond. Scott Adams and Frank Bell were two of the carpenters. The sand for the fireplace came from sand cove and was taken over in a scow.

About 1875, spruce, fir, and pine was cut along the shore of the pond: there was a dam built at the head of the pond outlet and logs were drove down the outlet to the East Branch. One can still see where the earth was removed and used in the dam.

▲ *Original dining hall on waterfront (Courtesy of the Edwards Family)*

In 1910, a fish screen was installed in the outlet and the pond was stocked with some landlocked salmon. Two years later, Mr. Cornelius Lane had some small-mouth bass shipped to him and put in the pond.

A Mr. Whitney bought a lot of land and made a clearing on the south side of Pleasant Pond and built a house and barn. When he moved away, about 1900, he sold to John Lane. It is now referred to as Whitney Point. Mr. Joseph Edwards, the Civil War veteran, would swim some of his young stock across the pond in the spring and pasture them there, after Whitney left the place.

In 1929, my father and George Dow, my cousin, went up to the Oxbow to look at some log cabins to get an idea how to construct them. They built the first one that summer and thought it quite a building. It was 24 feet x 16 feet, and is still in use today: Cabin #4. Ralph, Daniel, Scott Adams, and I cut logs and would build one every summer for six or eight years. Joe Edwards, Dannie, and Keith put a cement wall under them in 1965—so that they could be used in the fall and winter. About this same time, Joe installed oil heat in all of them and rented two or three of them to the Maine Starch Company, who had a factory in Island Falls.

Many people from the area would come to the pond in the winter and fish smelt; they were very plentiful as well as cusk. The fisherman

The Edwards Family, 1948 Left to right, back: Ralph, Joseph, Father (W. F.), Mother (Melvina), Julia Front row: William Jr., Sheppard, Danny, Lawrence, and Keith (Courtesy of the Edwards Family)

would get the old cedar rails and use them for a wood fire. They were from George Walker's cedar fence.

During the winter of 1954 to 1955, the dance hall went down from too much snow on the roof. Also in 1955, Joe Edwards dismantled the old lunch room which was built in 1931 and constructed the new lodge, which is still there. He and his wife, Delma, had had been living at the farm until then. Seems to me that Joe said it cost him about $80,000, which he borrowed from the bank. In 1960, the cold winter, he bought some used bowling alley in Caribou and had it installed in the basement. This proved to be a very good investment for him. Previous to this, one had to go to Houlton to do any bowling. The summer people were still coming to the Point and staying in the camps and getting their meals at the lodge. The campground for the campers was opened in 1964 and has been very successful; all of which represents a lot of work through the years. The laundromat and shower room was built in 1965. The brothers Danny, Ralph, Lawrence, and myself all tried to help on these projects all we could.

My father, William Edwards Sr., moved the family to Island Falls in 1921 so the children could go to school; before this Shepard, Lawrence, Danny, and Ralph drove to school in the winter with a horse and sleigh. Mother worried about them as a lot of the time. It was dark when they got home, and the kids would be real cold. Father worked in the potato house for George York, and we would move back to the farm in the spring about the 1st of May. This same procedure took place for several years. First house we lived at was the old Britton moccasin factory, which is now gone, just the other side of the present Scott Dunphy house.

—KEITH EDWARDS

CHAPTER 4

Family Friends to All— George Dow and Philip Powers

GEORGE Dow was to everyone he knew, their favorite uncle, surrogate father, best friend, and teacher. A lover of life, he inspired many with his hunting and fishing stories.

◀ *Clockwise from left: Faye Dow, Keith Edwards, Delma Edwards, George Dow, Joe Edwards, Jean Edwards, Herb Hanson (Courtesy of the Edwards Family)*

He knew every rock and cranny of the pond, and the land around it. He was immensely patient with me and taught me much of what I know today about the natural wonder of the pond and the woods. We spent many hours and days together fishing, identifying, and always, eventually catching the big ones. He helped me through some very difficult times, gently and kindly. My father also viewed George as a father figure, as did Joe Edwards Sr. One of my goals in life is to pass on to my boys the sensibility and the love and the lore George expressed so effortlessly. I was 9 when George died, but I will always remember him as one of the most positive influences in my life.

—PHILIP A. POWERS

▶ Richard Armstrong
has the Dow Log
Cabin now through
a friendship with
"Uncle Jack"
(Photo by Sandra
Newman)

George worked many years as Maine's Potato Inspector, traveling the roads from Maine to Florida, but his true love was Pleasant Pond. Once he retired, George worked with Joe helping to build Birch Point and maintain the camps. He also worked as a fishing guide, guiding the guests staying in the cottages, teaching them the pond. "He caught one of the largest salmon from the pond, weighing in at 12 pounds," explained Joe. Joe's being second at 9 pounds.

George married Nel Dow and never had children, but this didn't stop them from having their friends' children become theirs. Joe and the Powers remember George and Nel as their second set of parents. Unfortunately for everyone, Nel passed away at a very young age. When George passed away, the Powers had a plaque made and placed it in the apple orchard that the Edwards planted overlooking Birch Point.

▶ The George Dow
Apple Orchard
(Photo by Sandra
Newman)

▶ George Dow
memorial headstone
(Photo by Sandra
Newman)

PHILIP L. POWERS took over managing the Martha A. Powers Trust when his father, Walter Powers, passed away in the late 1960s. His children remember their father loved the land and the pond more than anything: his joy of spending many weeks each summer at the old hunting camp. Never without a project, and some were quite ambitious, according to his sons, especially from Philip A.'s vantage point, working as a (usually) willing participant, in the days before they had a tractor. They built many things by hand, including the old dock that required cribs filled with boulders and the wharf house whose logs young Philip peeled and dragged to the site with chains.

Philip A. has said, "It was great-grandfather Powers fervent desire to keep the area as a natural preserve, the timberland acquired while governor, undeveloped." It was Philip's great-grandfather who often wrote about this land as his "natural gem."

Joe Edwards remembers Philip Powers was a very special, loyal, and trusted friend. Joe remembers receiving a telephone call in 1993, there had been a death in the Powers Family. Knowing it was Philip, he was greatly saddened. That fall, members of the Powers Family, including Philip A.'s mother, Joe, and his son, Joey, went to the Powers Camp by boat and scattered Philip's ashes under the pine tree on Pine Point.

▲ *Philip Powers (Courtesy of the Edwards Family)*

◀ *Pine Point at sunset (Courtesy of the Powers Family)*

▶ *Two chairs
(Photo by Sandra
Newman)*

CHAPTER 5

Oldest Camps on Pleasant Pond

Seth Campbell's sailboat (Courtesy of Island Falls Historical Society)

Before camps were built on the Pleasant Pond, people came to the pond to escape the summer heat and relax by spending those beautiful, warm, sunlit days paddling canoes, sailing boats, or swimming in the crystal clear water. It was an idyllic time to leisurely picnic at the public picnic area while enjoying the cool breezes off the water. About 1904, the idea of owning a piece of the pond became reality when Camp Lafalot was built.

(This picnic area was located where the new Longstaff Camp has been built on the north side of the south shore.)

CAMP LAFALOT, THE CRABTREE CAMP

Samuel Crabtree built the Crabtree Camp in 1904. It is the oldest standing camp on the pond.

Camp Lafalot, built 1904 (Courtesy of Island Falls Historical Society)

▲ *Samuel Crabtree (Courtesy of Island Falls Historical Society)*

Sam Crabtree, the druggist of the one and only drugstore ever in Island Falls, married Margaret Kelly and together they had 3 children: Paul, a state senator; Leah (Emerson), the first woman to be the Director of the Board of Education of Maine; and Sam, the first high school principal of Island Falls and a state representative.

Mary Ella Crabtree, Paul's daughter, married Morrison Robinson, an Episcopal minister, and they had 2 sons: Jonathan and David. While David, a school teacher, never married or had children, Jonathan had 3 children: Mark, David, and Kristen. Only Mark married, and had 3 children: Seth, Samuel, and Christian. Seth has married Melissa, and they have the 6th-generation child, Jackson, at the camp. Mark claims, "I was 2 weeks old when I first came to Camp Lafalot." He has inherited the camp from his father, who had inherited from his father.

Mark proudly points out there have been very few updates. "At one time there was a barn on the property. One side kept the family horse and buggy, and the other side served as the ice house. The porch, since been removed, served as the summer kitchen. There is now running water, electricity, and a bathroom. The outhouse is the bathroom. We replaced the floor, took out the box, and put the toilet in the outhouse!"

Electric heat was added when Morris, around 24 years old, was struck with polio and moved to camp. His father, Paul, would come every day and carry Morrison into the pond to exercise his legs. After recovering from polio, he continued to walk with a limp and used a cane. Overcoming these adversities, he went on earn a doctorate from Tufts University and became a minister in Lincoln, Massachusetts.

Mark Robinson's 7x-great grandfather, Agren Crabtree, was the captain of the privateer Harlequin which snuck out of the Machias River, and shot the first naval shot of the Revolutionary War at a British frigate.

—MARK ROBINSON

▲ *Crabtree plumbing*

◄ *Mary Ella Crabtree (Courtesy of the Crabtree Family)*

◄ *Mary Campbell (front), Lydia Banton (middle), Hope Hawkes, Al McLeod, Julia Crabtree (back) (Courtesy of Island Falls Historical Society)*

◄ *Crabtree party at Camp Lafalot for Centennial Celebration of Island Falls, Maine, 1972 (Courtesy of Island Falls Historical Society)*

THE HILLMAN CAMP

Hillman Camp, built 1907 (Courtesy of Pam Oliver)

The Hillman camp on Crabtree Lane was built in 1907, according to my father, Thomas Hillman, by his father, Harold C. Hillman. Harold Hillman received the land from Mr. W. Edwards as payment for blacksmithing jobs on the Edwards Farm. I do not know what year this happened, sometime before 1907. The land was deeded to my grandmother, Mary Sewall Hillman, in 1914, after my grandfather disappeared while acting as a deputy and serving a warrant on some bootleggers. The camp has been in our family ever since. According to my father, Thomas, it was the second oldest camp on the pond. What made the camp unusual was that it was built of upright poplar logs, and it had an interestingly shaped porch. It was never modernized.

The camp was in poor condition and was torn down. A new camp is being built in its place using some of the original timbers. It is expected to be completed during the summer of 2010.

I have many fond memories of the summers my brother and I spent on the pond, and I look forward to the present generation enjoying it as we used to.

—PAMLA HILLMAN OLIVER

Tingley Cottage, possibly the oldest (Photo by Sandra Newman)

THE TINGLEY COTTAGE

Another cottage to be considered in this cluster is the Tingley Cottage. Originally built as the one-room Walker-Edwards-Lane School in 1885, it was later moved to its present location around 1890 by a Mr. Cromment. This just might be considered the oldest camp on the pond.

CHAPTER 6

Overnight Cottages on Pleasant Pond

FISHER'S LOG LODGE AND LOG CABINS

Fisher Log Lodge (Photo by Sandra Newman)

The Fisher's Log Lodge and Log Cabins were originally built and operated by Reginald Fisher. In 1983, Marion and Robert McCaffery purchased the property the sons inherited. If you visit Fisher Log Lodge, you just might meet Bob and Paul McCaffrey and find them working at "camp maintenance." Interestingly enough, Marion Walsh McCaffery is Joanie MacAuliffe Walsh's sister-in-law who, with her brother, Joe, own Camp Theodore Roosevelt. The pond community truly is a close knit one.

CAMP THEODORE ROOSEVELT

▶ *Camp Theodore Roosevelt log cabin (Courtesy of Island Falls Historical Society)*

▲ *Canoes on Pleasant Pond by Camp Theodore Roosevelt (Courtesy of Island Falls Historical Society)*

F. Joseph "Mac" McAuliffe was teaching in Dorchester, Massachusetts, living in Wakefield, Massachusetts, and spending his summers, 1923 to 1927, working as a camp counselor for Theodore Roosevelt Boys Camp on Mattawamkeag Lake. It was during this time that he discovered his special cove "in the Maine woods on beautiful Pleasant Pond…I believe one of the most beautiful spots on the Pleasant Pond."

With his summers off and Camp Roosevelt on Mattawamkeag Lake no longer active, Mac established his own boys' camp, receiving his retailer's certificate June 1, 1928, for Camp Theodore Roosevelt. Ed Olson, a summer pond neighbor, and superintendent of schools in Lyndhurst, New Jersey, was one of his counselors.

DINING HALL, CAMP ROOSEVELT, NEAR ISLAND FALLS,

◄ *Camp Theodore Roosevelt dining hall (Courtesy of Island Falls Historical Society)*

The camp continued until the Depression when families were no longer able to spare the expense of sending their children to summer camp. It was then converted into an "overnight spot for families, with meals." Stella (McNally), Larlee and Leona (Albert Byron) were two of the waitresses and chambermaids. Don Myrick was a cook. Ed Quinlan Jr. was a groundskeeper, and Scott Adams supplied the trout. The Lane children from the top of the hill worked there, along with the Yorks and many Island Falls residents.

Mac McAuliffe was responsible for bringing many of the summer families to the area, bragging about his beautiful spot. Edward Quinlan Sr. was a lawyer in Boston when "Mac" was a teacher in Dorchester. Commuting to work together, Mac constantly bragged to Ed, "What a beautiful place I own in northern Maine." Ed became so intrigued that he brought his family to Mac's beautiful spot for a holiday and eventually, enjoying the area so much, moved his family to Island Falls. To make this move, both Ethel and Ed Quinlan had to give up their Boston law practices. Yes, Mrs. Quinlan, the Island Falls High School business teacher who taught us typing!

During World War II, the U.S. Air Force–Houlton Barracks took

CAMP THEODORE ROOSEVELT

ESTABLISHED—JUNE 1, 1928

1928—A CAMP FOR BOYS
1938—FAMILY —AMERICAN PLAN
1943—BARRACKS FOR USAF—HOULTON AFB
1946—FAMILY CAMP—HOUSEKEEPING CABINS
     OWNERS/PROPRIETORS
F. JOSEPH "MAC" MCAULIFFE—1928 (BUILDER)
MAC AND MARIE MCAULIFFE—1940
JOE AND SUE MCAULIFFE—1984
ED AND JOANIE WALSH—1984

▶ *Commemorative*
plaque hanging
in Joe and Susie
McAuliffe's cabin

over Camp Roosevelt. The officers lived in the cabins and the soldiers camped in John Lane Field. After the war, Camp Roosevelt became housekeeping cottages without meals, as it continues today with Joe and Susie McAuliffe, Joe's sister, Joanie McAuliffe Walsh, and family members responsible for Camp Roosevelt's success.

CHAPTER 7

The Lane Property Today

*Welcome to
Roosevelt Road*

THE PARKER CAMP

Ted and Cappy Parker built their little red camp in the 1960s along with their daughters, Linda and Gail, and son, Craig. They all moved from Oakfield, Maine, each summer to enjoy days basking in the sunshine. Linda and Gail were occasionally discovered floating "asleep" down the pond on rubber rafts. The tradition continues with their own grandchildren and various friends.

The Newmans and Parkers became fast and lasting friends, remembers Dr. Newman. "We had the property next door before we bought our camp, and the girls would camp out knowing full well if it rained, the Parker door was always open and they could go inside, in the middle of the night, to get out of the rain. Life on the pond is like living in a big family. I remember this camp with fun and fond memories."

THE KELLY CAMP

This little red camp was originally built by Bud and Nadine O'Roak from Sherman who later sold to Joe Kelly. Joe now spends his summers on the pond and the golf course.

▲ *Kelly Camp*

THE APPLEGATE/PACKER COTTAGE

▶ *Packer Cabin*

Like many of the original cabins on the pond, this was built using logs from the surrounding area. This cozy cabin maintains its delightful character with the most basic updates: electricity, water, and a road.

This is the cabin Edward Quinlan Sr. moved his family into when he first moved from Boston to Island Falls and worked at Camp Theodore Roosevelt.

THE OLSON COTTAGE

Mr. and Mrs. Edwin Olson built and summered in the Olson Cottage after purchasing the land from John H. Lane in 1939. Their daughter, Pat Olson, inherited the camp upon her parents' death, and now her son, Carl, spends his summers here.

I remember Mrs. Olson with fond memories of fresh chocolate chip cookies, homemade lemonade, and rainy afternoons. To savor such delectable treats, I would ride my bicycle to her camp, listen to Camelot on her antique victrola, and munch happily on cookies. Mesmerized, I was, by her stories. I spent many afternoons listening to "Mab" Olson's memories of her youth.

▲ *Olson Cottage*

THE DANIELS CAMP

This camp was built by Dr. and Freddie Daniels of Sherman, and is now occupied by their son and daughter-in-law, Bill and Diane (Porter) Daniels.

◀ *Daniels Camp*

THE WALKER CAMP

Built by Jesse "Red" Hoar, the Walker Camp was later sold to Mr. and Mrs. Gerry Bradbury from Fort Lauderdale, Florida, Richard Armstrong's father-in-law. The Bradburys later sold to Steve and Bebe (Hunt) Walker, who have made it into their beautiful year-round home. Before Steve and Bebe purchased this camp, they had spent many summers at Camp Roosevelt.

▲ *Steve and Bebe Walker Camp*

THE GRAY COTTAGE

This very cute year-round cottage was originally built by Owen Prince for his wife, Mildred, and their two daughters, Nancy and Mary. They enjoyed spending their summers on the pond. When Mildred passed away, Owen never returned to the cottage. This was when George Larlee, who owned Camp Camelot, approached Owen about selling the cottage to Dawn Marie and Mike LePlante. Dawn Marie loved the cot-

▶ *Gray Cottage*

tage and being on the pond, but Mike wasn't so content. They sold to the present owners, Cindy and Richard Gray.

Pond people have connections. This is how you might find your special place. Seems Dawn Marie's mom was George Larlee's wife's sister, and when she found out the cottage was for sale she just had to tell someone, "Who else but Barbara Crandall, who just happens to be Cindy Gray's mother."

THE BRODEAU LOG CABIN

The Brodeau log cabin at one time was owned by the Browns from Oakfield, Maine.

THE NEWMAN CAMP

◀ *Newman Camp*

Similar to the lots on Roosevelt Road and many lots all around the pond, this property was purchased from John H. Lane. Whenever John Lane needed money, he sold a piece of the pond to willing waterfront buyers. In 1950, Hope Hawks purchased Lot #4 and built this camp. She sold to Joy Newman in 1964. "I remember the excitement of moving to camp for the summer. Packing up on Memorial Day, along with many other lake and pond people, we'd move to camp for macaroni-salad summers of swimming, water skiing, bathing in the lake, not combing your hair, possible sunshine, and loads of friends…just plain fun! Mom (Joy Newman) always claimed she could tell a pond kid by their haphazard appearance!

School kids living on the pond would ride the school bus to and from the Point. Somehow they would make their way back to camp at the end of each day, having caught a ride in a boat at the Point or walked back for a late afternoon swim or waterski.

Being from the "lower end," we walked, which was thought the best because we were able to walk in front of all the camps. We caught up on local gossip, meandered here and there, and just took our time getting back with a rest stop at the forbidden McAuliffe's Apple Orchard. "Sorry Mac, I must confess, we picked a few!"

Can you imagine, the Delong kids lived across from the Point year-round and had to take their boat across "the way," sometimes barely meeting the bus! Just envision, ice-encrusted faces and freezing during the morning boat ride just to catch a school bus! And the Bowers? They have to make it up over their hill, for their ride to school in Houlton, Maine!

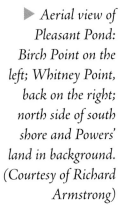

▶ Aerial view of Pleasant Pond: Birch Point on the left; Whitney Point, back on the right; north side of south shore and Powers' land in background. (Courtesy of Richard Armstrong)

THE KINNEY CAMP

Patti Desmond Hartin remembers, with these pictures, the Kinney Camp on Pleasant Pond.

◀ *Role Kinney with his 8½-pound, 10½-pound, and 15-pound 2-ounce brown trout (Courtesy of Patti Hartin)*

The pictures are of my grandfather, Roland Kinney Sr., with his fish: On the left is Role with his 8½-pound brown trout caught on Pleasant Pond in 1956. On the right is Role with his 10½-pound brown trout caught on May 20, 1962; it was 29-inches long. His 15-pound 2-ounce brown trout caught on May 21, 1962, was 30-inches long and had a girth of 21 inches. These fish were the biggest ever landed on the pond. I don't know if that record still stands. He got a mention in Field and Stream *magazine for the 10 and 15 pounders.*

—PATTI DESMOND HARTIN

THE ALBRIGHT CAMP

This camp was built by Smokey James of Oakfield, who sold to the Burpee Family. When Dick Albright got the idea to purchase a camp on the pond, he found this camp was for sale and bought it sight unseen. This is another camp rebuilt into a wonderful year-round home.

IN BETWEEN COTTAGES

Between the Albright Camp and Larlee's Hideout there are three cottages: The Sprague Log Cabin, The Timmin's year-round home, and Camp Camelot George Larlee. George Larlee was the brother of Frank Larlee who built the original Hideout.

THE HIDEOUT

▶ *The Hideout in the winter (Courtesy of Bruce Larlee)*

John H. Lane, son of Cornelius, sold the land where Bruce and Marge Larlee have built their year-round home to Ester Tewksbury in 1935. The original log cabin, The Hideout, was sold to Bruce Larlee's grandparents, William and Ola, in 1949. In 1978, their son, Frank, and his wife, Stella, purchased the cabin, and in 1987 Bruce and Marge took over The Hideout.

CHAPTER 8

Your Stories and Memories

Around the 1860s, families moved to northern Maine for many reasons. They came to avoid being shanghaied onto British ships sailing down from Canada and being taken off to fight battles in far-off lands. They came to settle on newly opened up land after the bloodless 1839 Aroostook War was settled by the Webster-Ashburton Treaty in 1842. And they came to take advantage of land grants being offered with the passing of President Abraham Lincoln's Homestead Act of 1862. They came because it was there. For whatever reason, they came to find a place to call home. Home for some ended up being Pleasant Pond.

Our pond may be small, but it's our magical pond; our Pleasant Pond. These are your stories and those of "the pond." I hope all that contributed and all that read these realize how special "our pond" truly is. Special thanks to the Powers Family for maintaining the Powers Trust and protecting what we all hold so dear and to everyone who lives and plays on "our pond,"

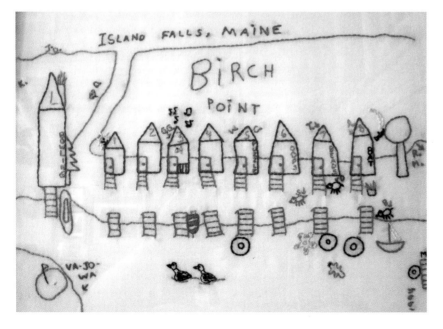

Drawn by Roger Tufts, age 5, embroidered by Merry Tufts, age unknown (Courtesy of Tufts Family)

for keeping it our special place. Our small but magical Pleasant Pond.

My sincere gratitude, love, and a heartfelt thank-you to all who contributed to this project and for letting me bug you for information.

LOSING YOUR BATHING SUIT

▲ *Packer road sign*

I have hundreds of great memories and experiences at Pleasant Lake that I reflect on often. Most of them are family memories with my grandparents (Frank and Dot Applegate) and my parents (Dave and Jane Packer). Our cabin has been my summer vacation spot for fifty years, since I was months old. I can truly say that the cabin and the lake are my "happy places."

I have vivid memories of camping with Gary, Diane, and Marci Pankratz, along with my sister, Sue, and brother, Jim. We camped on the islands and at the end of the lake and did a lot of things we weren't supposed to do!! Many times we would walk to Birch Point and play pinball for hours. We got so good at the machines we often played for free and racked up lots of wins.

One of my funniest memories (it's funny now) was also very embarrassing. I was dating a guy named Tim from Presque Isle, and he came to Pleasant Lake with a friend to spend the day. He brought along scuba equipment, and a big group of us went to Barker Rocks to test out the gear. Having only snorkeled before, I was excited to be able to go deep underwater. We were all taking turns, and when it was my turn, I suited up and took the plunge. I was in my mid teens and was wearing a string bikini (thank goodness someone has since invented the "tankini"). I tooled around for awhile underwater, exploring around the big rocks and spotting a few bass. After awhile I stood up on an underwater rock that was quite a ways out, lifted my mask and started waving back to all my friends who were sunning on Barker Rocks. All of them slowly started waving, then laughing, and pointing at me. Clueless, I waved enthusiastically back at them, but they all continued to laugh hysterically at me. After standing there for awhile I finally looked down and saw that my bikini top had disappeared during my dive. Panicked, I plunged back underwater and wondered how much air I had left while I frantically searched for my bathing suit top. After several more minutes I still couldn't find my top and wondered what I was going to do. There were no good options. Finally, I caught a glimpse of my top floating around my neck, where it had apparently been all that time, but had been floating behind me. I managed to get it back on without having to surface first, but I remember being extremely embarrassed and not wanting to come out of the water. Finally, I came out to more laughter, but some of it was from me too. When I try to picture myself then, I come up with a small-chested topless teenager, with a diving mask askew and a bikini string around my neck, not a pretty picture!

—MARY PACKER ARDIZZONE

SUMMERS IN THE COVE

Ah memories. It wasn't much of a camp, but its location for a young girl was great. Next door was my cousin Marcia Webb, and two doors was Aunt Blanche and Uncle Jim. And the last camp on the cove was Aunt Rena and Uncle Leo Bishop. It was this wonderful A-Fame, and they had a boat that I thought was the hippest thing on the pond.

One of my best memories is the "bed swing" on our front porch facing the lake. It hung from the rafters, a full-size bed, which you could swing on especially in the early morning hours, listening to the cry of the loons. At night, it became a magical place, watching lights dance off the water across the way, or a storm move in, with lightening lighting up the skies, the breeze off the water that would blow the red curls and make them dance.

Of course in my early teenage years it was the best place because of the family across the cove. The James family! Lots of kids, but one very special young boy whom I was madly in love with in those summer years, Gary.

I was lucky enough to have an old row bow that we would all pile into and go fishing there in the cove, catching mostly sunfish. On other days when we were bored, we'd row over to Swett's Cove to see what we could catch there. Gary loved to sing, so at dusk most nights we would sit out in the middle singing and harmonizing until our vocal cords cried, no more.

My Grandmother (Ida Hoar Edwards)

▼ *(Photo by Sandra Newman)*

lived up the hill with her husband, Danny, who was so good to me. One summer he presented me with a small aluminum boat and a 10-horse power engine (and all the gas I wanted). I thought I'd died and gone to heaven. As long as I acted responsible with it, it was mine for as long as I could use it. (This was for a number of years) What a gift. I now had the chance to go way down the lake to my Aunt Mary and Uncle Charlie Sprague's camp or to Barker Rocks and Sand Cove. Oh freedom!

Just off of our dock was an old float held up by barrels. Marcia and I would swim out to it every day, Gary, his brothers and sisters would meet us there. We would spend hours pushing, shoving each other off into the water, playing king/queen of the float. Swimming underneath it from one side to the other to do a sneak attack was great (also where my first kiss took place).

One summer the old barrels had rusted, so Marcia and I decided it needed repairing. We found some new barrels, but could not figure out how to make them stay put. I came up with the idea of using rope. Not a good idea. I kept diving with the rope hoping to secure the barrels. On my final trip underneath I became trapped. Thank goodness Marcia was there as she finally got me out just as I thought I'd be taking my last breath! (WHEW) Needless to say we let the adults fix it.

Swimming lessons were offered at the Point for a number of years. I had actually worked my way up to Life Saving. Our teacher was Mr. Mayberry the year that I took this class. What a great teacher, but the tests we had to pass were awful. I will never forget when it was Sandy Newman's time to do "the rescue" of a drowning victim. He held her under, next thing you knew up she came with a huge scream and Mr. Mayberry a bit worse for wear. Ouch!

—SHARMAN (HOAR DREW) BALL

GOOD OLD JOE

Since we purchased our camp on the pond in 1986, ice fishing has been an integral part of our family life. We've progressively gotten better at ice fishing as the years have passed. From those flimsy green tip-ups to poly- hardwood Mooseheads; pull-sleds to a fancy dogsled; chisels to two Eskimo ice augers; aerated bait buckets; and state-of-the-art clothing and gloves. From the warmth of the sun room, we could easily tend traps in shirt sleeves on the coldest days.

Smelting was also a favorite pastime, and when Steve Greenlaw disposed of his shack, we were lost, so I decided to build one. However, I knew that my sons, Chris and Jeff, would be somehow unavailable when it came time to bring it on and take it off the ice. Due to the close quarters around the camp and the steep bank in front of it, the standard shack just wouldn't cut it, even if they did help. It had to be something I could handle myself. So I had to dream up something unique.

After much contemplation and daydreaming, I decided it had to be round so I could tip it over and roll it. Important design criteria: strong—able to withstand abuse; easy to heat; roomy—must seat six comfortably; removable floor plates for smelt lines; and all the bells and whistles imaginable. Four months of design and build work in my Bangor garage produced an 8-foot diameter x 78-inch high round insulated ice shack made from galvanized metal roofing complete with Lexan windows and safety reflectors. It was the talk of the Fairmount neighborhood—lots of stopping and starting. So in November 1998, Chris and I loaded it in the back of his truck, and off we went to Island Falls. I can't imagine what people thought as they whizzed by us on I-95.

As we drove up the Pond Road I said to Chris, "Let's see what old Joe thinks of it." After all, who would be more qualified to evaluate this masterpiece than Joe….think of all the shacks he had built over the years. So

▲ Ice fishing on Pleasant Pond

we pulled into the parking lot at the Point, and out came Joe. I was beaming with pride as he asked me what it cost to build it—I replied, "about 400 bucks, so what do you think?" He slowly lumbered around the truck bed, carefully scanning the construction and only in a way an honest, salt-of-the-earth guy from Aroostook County could answer: "Well Bruce a fool and his money are soon parted." Talk about air out of a balloon, but Joe's still one of my favorites.

—BRUCE BOISVERT

BANGOR MAILMEN

The winter of 1991 was very unusual—lots of very cold days followed by warm days of driving rain and then back to sub-zero the next day. On one of those "quick change in the weather" weekends, Pleasant and Mattawamkeag saw at least eight vehicles (three within view of our camp) break through the ice in as much as 4 feet of water—the lakes were dotted with valleys caused by ice settling from the weight of the heavy rains. An early morning snow storm masked the location of these "dipsies."

Pulling my Polaris out of the water that morning and helping another snowmobiler who had sunk up to his waist with his brand new Ski-Doo, was enough excitement for one day. This required eight of us with a 50-foot-long rope pulling for all we were worth—we couldn't get near the hole because the ice kept breaking away. However, the best was yet to come that night with another snow squall and brutal cold. Around 10:00 p.m. we were surprised to hear a knock on the door.

Two Bangor mailmen, both exhausted and covered with snow head to foot explained they had broken through the ice (around 300 yards out from Roosevelt Cove). The owner of the SUV was particularly bummed because he had just purchased it. We could see the dim headlights pointed skyward in the distance. He asked to use my phone...sure. To my surprise, he called the warden (John Fowler, I believe). He explained he paid State of Maine taxes and had a valid fishing license and wanted his vehicle off the lake immediately! I'm not sure what the warden said but I think it went something like—"You will get the vehicle out and you will pay all of the costs."

A very panicky postman asked me if I knew of anyone who could get the car off the ice because it would surely freeze in solid that night. Anybody familiar with this lake knows the only one that could help in this situation would be Joey Edwards.

Don't ask me how, but Joey did get the car off that night, and it was hauled to Porter's where it stayed until it thawed out the next day.

—BRUCE BOISVERT

MY BEGINNER SWIMMING CLASS

I remember taking swimming lessons the summer of 1964, and riding on the bus with Leo Bishop driving. We sang, and sang, and really must have driven Leo crazy with our song selections." We sang *Oh! Susanna*, and *The Bus Goes Round and Round*, with everything sung in rounds. I remember Danny Joy and I tried harmonizing with great success!

▲ *Birch Point sign, where Red Cross swimming lessons were held until 1965.*

I had decided I needed to learn to swim at the great impressionable age of 14. I signed up, showed up and discovered I was to be in a Beginner Class full of 7 year olds! At the time, the situation was very distressing, but now kind of funny. Since I already knew how to put my face in the water, and float, I breezed through beginners and quickly advanced to Advanced Beginners with pride.

—WINNIE (WHITE) DESMOND

THE HONEYMOON AT CAMP OBO

Claudine and Owen Dow were married in 1935, in Millinocket, Maine. They honeymooned at his Uncle Wills Edwards third cabin at Birch Point on Pleasant Pond. In 1950, Owen Dow and his father-in-law, Bowman McLain, and Marshal Hall built his camp. Owen and Claudine lived in Sherman Station, Maine, he owned a drug store. They were at camp all summer with their children, Bill and Jane, for many years. The camp, in the cove, is still in full swing as Dean and Jane

Camp OBO, built 1950 (Courtesy of Jane Fitzgerald)

Fitzgerald have it now.

Dean and Jane were married October 19, 1963. They went away for a few days to the White Mountains in New Hampshire before coming back to stay at the camp. One morning they woke up to find 3 to 4 inches of snow on the ground and quickly moved out. Retiring in 1997, they stay all summer at the camp moving home in the middle of October.

History repeats itself as their two children, David and Lynn, and family vacation there. Many relatives and friends still enjoy visiting.

—JANE DOW FITZGERALD

MEMORIES OF SMELT FISHING ON PLEASANT POND

Around December 1946, sometime after Christmas, the pond was frozen solid. The ice was hard and clear as glass and the smelt were biting. Our family lived in a house located at what is now #4 Green at Va-Jo-Wa Golf Course. Santa had been good to us Gerow children that year with plenty of goodies to please a 13 year old boy and his younger brother, Donald. Don was wicked proud of the scout knife he had received and I equally proud of the new sled.

It was a clear bright day. So a fishing trip to the pond was hurriedly planned. We grabbed a pail, a couple of lines, tackle, salt pork (for bait), Dad's axe, Don's new knife, and filled the pail half full of Christmas candy. We were going to make sure we had enough energy to pull the sled to the pond and back home again. The plan was to use the salt pork to catch the first smelt, then use Don's new knife to remove its throat, which made excellent bait to catch more smelt.

Upon arrival, I chopped a hole for Don about 30 feet in front of a smelt shanty owned by Joe Edwards. I was proceeding to chop another hole nearby when I heard Don utter a profanity. "What's the matter," I asked? "I just dropped my new knife down the hole," he whined.

We were fishing in about 20 feet of water, so my first thought was, "He can kiss that new scout knife good bye." "Hold on" I said, "I'll rig another line with a bigger hook and sinker and see if I can snag it." About a million to one shot I guessed, but nothing ventured, nothing gained. To our surprise, after finding the bottom of the pond, and giving the line a couple of jigs, I felt something like a fish on the line. Hand over hand the line was retrieved until onto the ice flopped, a brand new scout knife just as wet and cold as a smelt, but much more appreciated.

The smelts were biting that day and our pail was starting to fill up, when from the smelt shanty there was a loud clatter and "BANG," the door flew open. Out onto the ice bounced a VERY LARGE SALMON with a fisherman in full pursuit. He wrestled the fish to a standstill, pulled out his knife and cut its throat to quiet it down. He hurriedly placed it in a knapsack and immediately left.

Fast forward about fifty years. I was visiting my mother, Myrna Sleeper, and her husband, True, at their cottage on Mattawamkeag Lake. We had just come back from church in Island Falls when True suggested that we take a boat ride down to the Point to visit Wallace Townsend.

Wallace was making the coffee while I was occupying myself by looking at pictures hung around the camp. One picture caught my eye. It was a picture of Wallace holding up a VERY BIG fish. When I asked him about it, he told me this fascinating story about fishing smelts in Joe Edwards' shanty on Pleasant Pond when he hooked a VERY LARGE fish on a smelt line. He pulled the fish up into the long hole in the ice, at that point the fish started jumping all around, splashing cold water everywhere and shed the small hook in its mouth. He said, "I did the only thing I could do, I took a swipe at it with my rubber boot, connected like a football player kicking a field goal." "The fish hit the shanty door broadside pulling a small wire loose, releasing the door, and out onto the ice the fish flopped."

Wallace went to Bucky Webb's store and weighed the "catch" at a little over 10 pounds. Wallace didn't have to tell me all of the detail of this fish story because I was there that day, but now I know, "the rest of the story."

—WALLACE A. GEROW

A BYRON BOATING ADVENTURE

Growing up on "the pond" provided the Barons with hundreds of great memories. It truly was the best place to be during the summer. I have two childhood memories of boating incidents that took place when I was a child. One of them was very frightening; the other was an extreme encounter with black flies.

The first was an event that created sheer terror in a 5 year old. Many of you may remember the little red race boat my father had. The boat wasn't very big, was made of wood, and really only sat three people. Peter and I were about 5 and 7 when my father took us to the Powers' camp. My grandfather, Pete Michaud, was cooking for them while they were at their camp. It was a beautiful day when we left to go visit Grampy. However, coming home as we came out of the Powers' cove and rounded the Point we were faced with giant white caps and we were going against them. The boat was being hit by them head on, with water coming into the boat. I remember looking at my Dad, who was completely focused on steering the boat. After a few minutes he told us quite firmly to get under the deck, don't move and to stay put. Peter and I immediately did what we were told to do. It was a very scary ride, not only were we being slammed around, but we couldn't see anything. Being very young the ride seemed to go on forever. We finally made it home in one piece. It was then I realized just how scared my father was. Once we were out of the boat—he just sat on the wharf for a few minutes catching his breath. My mother came flying down the stairs to make sure we were all okay; thankfully we were.

The other event was another one that Peter and I were involved in. We were both pre-teens with access to a boat and a lake full of friends. The rule was that we could not go around Whitney Point without permission. Mom wanted to be able to see us. Well of course we didn't listen. It was a nice day so we decided to venture down to Sand Cove. From the cove we crossed over to Barker Rocks. After a spell we decided it best to return home, hoping Mom hadn't been looking for us. Not very far from Barker Rocks we ran out of gas. Fortunately, we had oar locks, and we

▲ *Peter Byron (Courtesy of Candy Guerette)*

were required to always take the oars with us. So we began to row. The lake wasn't very choppy, so we were making good progress. However, we were soon discovered by the black flies. Not just a few black flies, but swarms of black flies. We were rowing feverishly, trying to get away but to no avail. We just couldn't get ahead of them. After a half hour or so, we were both pretty well chewed up, and I was in tears. Finally a good Samaritan showed up and offered us a tow, which we gladly accepted. Once we were deposited on our wharf, we were left to deal with a very angry mother. However, I think both Peter and I welcomed the scolding as it wasn't nearly half as bad as the flies were.

—CANDY (BYRON) GUERETTE

BOAT RACES

For a number of years speed boat races were held on the pond. It was very exciting as buoys were placed around the lake. Crowds came from all around to see the hydroplanes skim across the water. The boat races were a big deal—all of the wharfs were crowded while boats filled with spectators were anchored all around the course. Peter, John, and I gathered on our wharf, which provided a perfect view of the races. We were stunned by just how fast these boats were. Our Dad had a speedboat that we thought was the fastest boat on the lake. These boats would have blown right past him. They zoomed around a course which is similar to the one currently being used for the canoe race.

One year as they were careening around the buoy, one of the hydroplanes became airborne, flipping over and dumping the driver. We waited tensely on our wharf for the rescue boat to retrieve him, which they did. The Cook Family would join us with our Dad providing a play-by-play of the action for us, so we could get a sense of what was going on. We all had favorites which we would cheer for. I'm sure some of the favorites were selected because of the style of the boat or the type of motor. Mine were selected because of their color.

—CANDY (BYRON) GUERETTE

MY SWIMMING LESSONS

My memories of Pleasant Pond are many. This is where I took swimming lessons as a child. We would all meet at the school ground and take the school bus (for 10¢) and be picked up and dropped off after our lesson. I remember the little changing house out in the middle of the area that is now a campground. There was a side for the girls and a side for the boys. The boys had a peep hole into the girls' side. They didn't think we knew it, but we did! We would stuff the hole with tissue paper long enough to change, but they would always knock it back out. After our swimming lesson, the kids that had a nickel would go to Joe Edwards' store close to the beach and get an ice cream cone. There was also a bowling alley downstairs at the store. That was a big thing to us back then. Shirley McNally and I walked all the way from Station Street just to go bowling one day!

There was, and still is, a camp right next to the store owned by the Tingley Family. The girls, Susan, Judy, and Barbie, lived next door to me, so I spent a lot of time at the camp with them. It was good swimming in front of the camp, and they also had a boat, which was a big thrill to ride in. Pleasant Pond was, and always will be, full of awesome childhood memories for me.

—DARLENE HARTIN

THE KINNEY CAMP

I have attached a few pictures from the Kinney Camp at Pleasant Pond. I have included a picture of Roland and Mona Kinney taken in front of the "garbage can tree" where they always tied up the can to keep the raccoons out. It was taken in 1966.

Also a couple of pictures of the "Kinney kids," Barbara, Ellen, and Joan Kinney, children of Roland Jr. and Nancy Kinney, and another of Barbara, Ellen, and Joan and Patti Kinney, and Phillip Desmond, Sike Desmond, and Joanne Kinney Desmond taken in front of the camp.

▶ *Roland and Mona Kinney (Courtesy of Patti Hartin)*

I could not find any pictures of the camp itself but what a nice camp it was. I have wonderful memories of sleeping out on the porch. We all would have to take turns because everyone wanted to sleep there. I was

◄ *Kinney Kids: Barbara, Ellen, and Joan (Courtesy of Patti Hartin)*

▼ *More Kinney Kids: Barbara, Ellen, Joan, Patti, and Phillip (Courtesy of Patti Hartin)*

afraid but didn't let on. The sound of the loons at night scared me, but I toughed it out. There was a bear-skin rug from a bear that my grandfather and my brother shot when it tried to climb into the boat (this is what my brother tells me and I have no reason to doubt it).

In the early years we had the Hope Hawks camp on one side of us and the Smokey James camp on the other. Soon the Newmans bought the Hope Hawks camp. I remember being allowed to walk out to the mailbox, which was out by Roosevelt Camps, and we thought we were "all that." We would stop by Mrs. Olsen's wonderful raspberry patch and sneak a few berries. When we were a bit older we could walk to Birch Point all along the shore or along the path in front of the camps. We memorized all the camps along the way. I still remember many of those names. Most have changed hands now. We had great fun when the Connecticut Kinneys arrived. My cousin Ellen always fell in the lake, strangely less than an hour after a meal, as we were not allowed to swim before that. I remember listening to the Red Sox on the radio. It was quiet time then, so my grandfather could hear the game. A special memory is of my Nana Kinney cooking breakfast.

She always had those little grapefruit sections, and cantaloupe served with soft boiled eggs. Those were the best! Of the few things we got from the camp when it was sold was a handmade braided rug Nana made. There were two of them in the camp, one in the kitchen and one in the living room, which was really one big room. I still have one in my home.

—PATTI DESMOND HARTIN

THE HUNT COTTAGE

(Photo by Sandra Newman)

It was 1945, and World War II had just ended. My father, Theodore E. Hunt (1919–1992) had returned home after serving three years in campaigns in Tunisia, Morocco, Algeria, Sicily, Italy, France, and Germany, with the First Armored Division, the 13th Airborne Division, and the First Allied Airborne Task Force.

His immigrant ancestor was Edmund Hunt, who had settled in Cambridge, Massachusetts, in 1634 and had moved to Duxbury, Massachusetts, in 1637.

He had recently married Margaret I. Doherty (1917–2001) of the Charlestown section of Boston, Massachusetts. Her immigrant ancestor was Patrick Joseph Doherty, who immigrated from Clonmany, Count Donegal, Ireland, to Boston, Massachusetts, in 1860.

They learned that John H. Lane Jr. had a cottage lot for sale on Pleasant Lake. They approached him about purchasing it, and he offered to sell it for $50. Not having $50, despite having served overseas for almost three years, he borrowed the $50 from my mother. The deed was drafted by Seth D. Campbell Esq., a graduate of Suffolk University Law School, August 20, 1945. He practiced in Island Falls from 1893 to 1951.

Prior to World War II, my father had owned a candy store in Island Falls, located at 5 Sherman Street. In 1949, the candy store was moved to the lot and became the first Hunt Cottage.

Our westerly neighbor was Earl V. Noyes, a World War I veteran, who was with Ancil Mitchell on April 18, 1917, when his leg was blown off in combat. Two of Mr. Mitchell's sons were killed in World War II, one on March 15, 1945, and one on May 20, 1945. Earl's daughter, Eda Noyes Phipps, was our friend and good neighbor for sixty years, until she died in 2009. She was married to Charles Phipps, a MIT graduate, and a World War II veteran. On the same day he was captured during the Battle of the Bulge, his brother was killed in combat. Their mother received two telegrams from the War Department on the same day.

Our easterly neighbor was Ira Tarbell, D.M.D., a Houlton native, and a World War II veteran. They rarely used the cottage, and it was eventually sold to Robert and Thelma Smith.

On July 6, 1973, Theodore E. Hunt conveyed the Hunt Lot to Patrick E. Hunt, and Rose Ann Hunt. Stuart H. White Esq., who attended Bowdoin College and was a graduate of the United States Naval Academy and the Harvard Law School, drafted the deed. Mr. White practiced in Island Falls from 1972 to 1974.

In 1983, Patrick E. Hunt and Rose Ann (Flynn) Hunt constructed the current Hunt cottage, a Dutch Colonial gambrel. Frank Violette, of Benedicta, constructed the foundation. Miles Grant of Island Falls did

▲ Loons Swimming in the Rain (Photo by Sandra Newman)

all of the excavation and constructed the new camp road. Marcel Perron of Billerica, Massachusetts, did the framing, roofing, siding, and exterior windows and doors in 14½ days with the help of Leon York of Island Falls. George Dubois and Robert Dunphy of Island Falls installed the plumbing. The wiring was completed by Peter Marston, of Sherman, Maine. The drywall was completed by Yale Stevens of Sherman, Maine. The interior finish was done by Raymond Dow of Houlton, Maine.

The Hunt Family, Patrick, Rose Ann, Eileen, Kevin, and Danny, moved in on December 23, 1983. It was -23° outside, and -23° inside the house.

The new camp road was named Bally Brien Road, after Bally Brien, Waterford, Ireland, the home of Rose Ann's father, Michael F. Flynn, (1901–1954) an Irish Republican Army hero, who immigrated to Yonkers, New York, in 1928. Bally Brien translates in Gaelic to, "road leading to the town of the Irish kings."

His wife was Rose F. Hammond (1908–2002), who immigrated to Yonkers, New York, from New Ross, County Wexford, Ireland, in 1929.

—PATRICK E. HUNT

SWETT'S COVE

Baptist Church baptisms, my children were baptized there.

—GAYLEEN LEAVITT

HAPPIEST PART OF CHILDHOOD

The happiest part of my early childhood was spending time in Island Falls with my Aunt and Uncle, Laura and Clyde Swett. The summers were the best. My earliest memory is getting into the small white rowboat at Birch Point and getting to the camp at night. Later a road was put in as far as the brook, and we walked in after dark. I remember spotlighting an owl in the tree. In those years, I would accompany Norman, who worked for the Swetts, to Birch Point in the rowboat to get ice for the ice box.

This beautiful log cabin named Lumbago Lodge was built by Dr. Swett

JUNE 18, 1914–
Twenty-four were baptized by Rev. E. M. Trafton at Pleasant Pond on Sunday. The day was an ideal one, and about 225 went from the village by teams and automobiles.

—SAMUEL R. CRABTREE
News Items

and helper, Vic, around 1936. The logs were all from the property. Dr. Swett was an expert with block and tackle. The beautiful stone fireplace was in the corner of the living room, with stone niches to hold interesting objects. The living room had three huge windows that overlooked the creek in the back that gave it its name. Beyond the creek was a badminton court made of sand, where we spent many happy hours. One of my earliest memories is standing near the brook and hearing the strains of *Sweet Georgia Brown* coming from the player piano. We spent hours at that piano and had a huge collection of rolls from the 1930s to 1950s.

A stairway of half logs, open between, led to two bedrooms and a large balcony. I slept in all these rooms over the years. My favorite place to sleep was the front porch which gradually went from just screens to windows. I loved to hear the music from dances at the pavilion at Birch Point. I never got to go to a dance there until 1956, with Richard Martin. We married in 2006.

All our meals were taken at the big table on the porch. What a great view. I loved the cows and their bells in their pasture across the lake; up the hill from Birch Point I could also hear the train in certain conditions. I was surprised the other day to hear the train from our cabin on the thoroughfare of Mattawamkeag Lake.

My favorite activity was swimming. Lying on the float and canoeing in the Old Town Sponson was also special. Tony Swett and I spent a lot of time in the Chris Craft Runabout terrorizing the lake I am sure. The Cabin Cruiser was also fun especially sitting on the front deck. One of my memory pictures is of Dr. Swett stepping from Grenier's dock to the boat and going straight down into the water and coming up with his cigar still clamped in his teeth.

Swett's Cove was open to the public for picnics. Uncle Clyde loved bonfires and was always burning brush, sometimes getting in trouble with the fire wardens. He loved a big bonfire. At one time he had a bowling alley and a sawmill with a track. The doctor devoted most summer mornings graveling the road, cutting wood, and working around camp. He loved to work. I loved to watch all the activities. One of the things he built was a bridge made of small cedar logs over the outlet from the spring. It had a bench and my mother could often be found there reading.

When I was 13 I went off with my sister to work in summer hotels. I seldom returned. My daughter and I skied in to the camp in the winter in the late '70s from Walkers. In 2006, I received a marriage proposal from

Dick Martin in the words, "Would you like to live in Island Falls?" I love to drive down to the pond, get water from the old spring, and take a dip in the wonderful, cold, clear water.

—DOTTIE ALFORD MARTIN

NOW THE SMELT STORY FOR YOU

When Richard Martin was about 11 years old, he used to hike down to the pond in the early morning, about 5:00 a.m., and use the fishing shacks that were open. One morning he went there, and in his excitement of tending two lines, he pulled up a line with fish on it, and after taking the fish off, he put the fish hook in his mouth to get the other line. The line froze in the hole, so when he moved his head it stuck in his lip. He walked up to Dr. Swett's office in Island Falls. "The good doctor" obligingly cut the hook out. The doctor said he would have to tell his dad. Richard said, "Doc, you can tell him anything you want; just give me a 20 minute head start to get back to the pond because the fish are biting." Richard proceeded to catch 189 smelt that morning.

—DOTTIE ALFORD MARTIN

RICHARD MARTIN'S OTHER STORY

This is before Dr. Newman arrived on the scene. Richard and his dad took the dog to Dr. Swett in the middle of the night, and he took out the porcupine quills. Richard says you never saw such a happy dog when he came out of ether. Now the center of Richard's life is his lovely orange cat with the white tip on his tail from the Newman collection.

—DOTTIE ALFORD MARTIN

IMPORTANT PART OF MY EARLY DAYS

AH!…Memories of Pleasant Pond…where do I start? Such a beautiful place and such an important part of my early days. I learned to swim there…Warren Walker took me for my first ever boat ride (scared me to death)…picnics with family and friends…always trying to go swimming on the first day of summer no matter how cold the water was…and IT WAS COLD!!!

Skinny dipping when I was 8 months pregnant…in the dark of

course! I used to babysit for Kirk and Margaret Palmer at their camp on the pond…and chasing after their five little boys sure kept me busy. Bowling at Birch Lodge…Hitching a ride there from town… usually with a bunch of kids… begging and teasing Mom and Dad…please take us swimming after supper…please…we'll be good…and always…you have to wait an hour after you eat! Somewhere in my things I have a picture of Matthew Roberts in swim trunks standing on the Point. I think it was a church picnic that we were at. So sad that he is now gone. I actually named my son after him.

—JENNIFER (MCGRAW) MCCOURT

▲ *Road signs on South Shore Road (Photo by Sandra Newman)*

REFORESTATION OF FARMS

In 1968, the U.S. government was giving pine tree seedlings to farmers to plant in fields they were no longer using. For a reforestation project, the farmers bought tree planting machines and replanted their fields. The Longstaff's planted their potato fields, and I planted the lot I had purchased on Pleasant Pond from Edward Quinlan Sr. in 1962. All the Pine Groves around Island Falls are the result of this reforestation program.

—DR. RAY C. NEWMAN

A BRIEF HISTORY OF OUR CAMP—63 ROOSEVELT ROAD

After many years of coming to Camp Roosevelt, run by the very nice McAuliffe Family, my father, Frank Applegate, bought our camp from Ed Quinlan Sr. in about 1950. It is a very old real log cabin. It was in primitive condition. It had no road, only a path from the main road. My father, being very handy, completely modernized the cabin by working on every vacation, and after his retirement, on all kinds of improvements.

I have been coming to the lake since age 5 and love it here. My three children all spent their summers here as they grew up. They learned to swim, fish, boat, and water ski. They were here from June to late August most years with my parents.

I hope that they, and also my grandson, will continue to enjoy the cabin as their "second home" for many years. We have made many good friends here through the years. Pat Olson, her son, Carl Kaestner, the McDonalds, the Pankratz Family on the south shore, and many others too numerous to mention. Several years ago two elderly men came by and said they had built our camp in the 1920s or 1930s. Other than that I don't know of its early history—how or exactly when it was built. Someone else may know more than I do of its beginning.

—JANE A. PACKER

ICE FISHING FOR SMELT

Early 1970, ice fishing for smelts and salmon. Levi King and Emile Robichaud, when times were slack, would go to the lodge (Edwards) and play cribbage with Keith Edwards. I think they just liked playing cribbage because Levi and Emile could catch smelts anytime they wanted. They had a knack for catching smelts.

—RALPH POWERS

THE WATER WAS SO COLD

"Cold water—the water was so cold! I would accompany my mother, "Tiny" Lake to Swett's Camp, and while she cleaned the camp, I would hang out with Kathy Numeryck. I remember we played records, sang, and went swimming." Now Val had taken swimming lessons at the Point, but never really learned to swim because the water was just a bit too cold. Determined she was to jump off the dock, "I held my nose, ran with all my might, and jumped in! I couldn't swim. I just sank to the depths of doom, and paddled with all my strength, to the top."

—VALERIE LAKE POWERS

BELIEVE IN MIRACLES

We were living summers at our camp on the south side of the pond, now known as South Shore Road. We had built it from the ground up, starting in 1969. My husband, Marty, age 38, was the main contractor, builder, and laborer, using plans from a book of vacation homes. He was assisted by our son Gary, age 12, daughter, Diane, age 9, and another daughter, Marcia, age 5. Also advice and labor was provided by his wife, Doris, age 38.

We worked on the camp every summer until it was pretty well finished in 2009, although it seems there is a new project going on each year. Our children enjoyed life on the pond—swimming, boating, water-skiing, snorkeling, fishing, etc. and also helping with work on the camp.

▼ *Pleasant Pond road signs (Photo by Sandra Newman)*

They grew up, went to college, left home, and settled in their own homes, in Texas, Kansas, and Michigan, but always loved coming to camp in Maine; they come now with friends and their own children.

One summer, June 2002, our son Gary, now age 44, came with his son, Taylor, age 15, to spend a couple of weeks. It was early in June, days were nice, but the water was cold. They decided to go to the islands near Sand Cove to swim. They took their small fishing boat and tied it up on the rocks on the second island. They swam around the island, then noticed the boat had come loose and was drifting out toward the outlet. Taylor started to swim for it but realized he couldn't make it so returned to the island. Gary then decided to try to get it, started out, but the boat was drifting further away. Gary was becoming exhausted in the cold water. He said he just couldn't move his arms and legs. Meanwhile Taylor was yelling for help. Down the lake about a half-mile, two fishermen had stopped their trip to the end of the lake to recover a submerged fishing rod. They heard Taylor yelling, but thought it must be kids playing at Sand Cove, then they realized it

▼ *Seagull Rock (Photo by Sandra Newman)*

was a call for help. They couldn't get their boat started, but eventually did start it and went to where Gary was in the water. The fishermen reached down and grabbed Gary by the hair and pulled him to the surface, where he said it was 40 foot deep. They didn't know how they could get him into the boat. At that moment, a man appeared in a canoe, jumped out, and helped hoist Gary into the fishermen's boat. They started for Birch Point; the fishermen had a cell phone with only 1 mark on it but they got through to call for an ambulance. They told them they thought Gary was dead, as he wasn't responding. When they got to Birch Point, they laid him on the bank and he regained consciousness, but complained of being hot. The ambulance took him to Houlton Hospital where he was admitted to ICU. He had been under water for some time. He was given IVs, but his kidneys were not functioning. After 4 days, the doctors decided to send him to Bangor to Eastern Maine Medical Center for possible dialysis. After 12 hours, without dialysis, his kidneys started to work, and he was discharged 2 days later.

Gary talked about the experience later. He said he knew he was going under and swallowing lots of water. He said he thought to himself, "If I am going to drown, this is a good place to die, here on the pond." We are so thankful that he recovered, and so thankful to the people who helped him. We do believe in miracles!

—DORIS PANKRATZ

PLANE CRASH

It was a dark and foggy night on August 14, 1988. We were at camp on the South Shore Road, which is next to the stream that comes down from Lost Pond. We heard a plane overhead, flying low and circling. It continued for a while, then apparently flew away. It was around 9:00 p.m.

The next morning, 9:00 a.m., it was still foggy—nothing but a white blur clear down to the ground. There was no visibility across the pond. We decided to go into town to get the mail. When we reached the Dow Farm Road, we saw lots of men standing and cars parked there. We found that folks on Mattawamkeag Lake had also heard the plane, and then heard a crash. Volunteers were joining together to form teams to search the surrounding area. Marty (Pankratz) joined a group headed by John Prescott. They met a group led by the Porters, who had started at the shore of Mattawamkeag Lake and worked up to Dow Farm Road. They found nothing, so Prescott's group went up from there toward Lost Pond. The area was rocky and hilly.

At 12:22 p.m., on August 15, 1988, the plane was found, crashed into a hemlock tree near the highest point from Lost Pond. The plane was vertical from the nose to tail. The pilot had fallen into the tail section, and was dead. However, his wife was still in her seat and alive. She had been there about 15 hours with a broken leg and other injuries. A helicopter was able to land in a small clearing along South Shore Road. The EMTs were then able to climb up the steep terrain and bring down the couple on stretchers. It was a couple from Castine who were flying north and lost their way in the fog. The wife was flown to Eastern Maine Medical Center where she was treated and released some days later.

—DORIS PANKRATZ

STREAKING

In the summer of 1972 or 1973, streaking was still a fad. My sons got my cousin Jack O'Donnell to streak the bowling alley at Birch Point. Brian was the scout, Doug the point man, and Mike the getaway driver. Anyway, Jack streaks across the alleys and up the stairs. Guess who's sitting at the counter? My daughter, Deidre, who was around 11 years old, calmly says, "Hi Jack."

—ED QUINLAN

LET'S GO HAWAIIAN

The invitation said, "Come in Your Most Creative Hawaiian Outfit." Mine was a skirt made from ferns picked alongside of our roadway, along with a Hawaiian shirt and a wide rim straw hat. Alice had a long skirt that she made with a Hawaiian blouse and the wide brim straw hat. Debbie Dwyer had a real Hawaiian skirt and a lei around her neck. We three tied for first place on the costume contest.

This contest was only a very small part of this friend-and-neighbors get-together sponsored by Brenda and Russ Rodgerson. They were wonderful host and hostess. I am told that they had been planning and preparing for this for a year. They had a gazebo set up with Hawaiian

◀ Annual Hawaiian Luau, Sand Trap Road; Front: Richard Rosen, Richard Burton; Table on left: Mary and Dick Elliot, Bob Miller, Nancy MacLean; Table on right: Bev Rand, Alice Briggs, Annie Townsend, Marge Larlee (Courtesy of Bev Rand)

lanterns and other Hawaiian decorations. The motif was distinctive and well done. Drinks and hors d'oeuvres were served. An experienced chef was roasting the pig. Others had been invited to bring in their favorite dish. Bruce Larlee brought his very good Bean-hole Beans. Judged by the very good food that was served, there were some excellent cooks around the shores of Pleasant Pond. It was all served in a leisurely fashion so that everyone enjoyed it. It was a fun family affair, as there were young folks as well as older. There were many photos taken by their son. These photos speak more for the occasion than the written word.

—BEV RAND

PLEASANT POND PIGLET

My father and I jointly bought our first cottage on Pleasant Lake in 1944, from the Keene sisters of Mars Hill, Maine. After a few years, my father suggested that I buy him out, and he would buy the cottage next door. We did that, and for quite a few years both families enjoyed the use of both of cottages. I was still farming, but we enjoyed the camp in the summer. We had many family gatherings here, which left us with special memories. One of those memories has to do with when we had the original camp. My brother from New York, my son, Stuart, and I got up one Sunday morning to go to the farm. We checked on Stuart's 4-H sow and found she had given birth to sixteen piglets. All but one was dead, and this one was cold and turning purple. My brother

*Bev Rand Camp
(Courtesy of
Bev Rand)*

grabbed it and tucked it under his jacket, and we headed to camp. My wife, Cora, took the piglet and placed it in a shoe box and put it in the oven of the wood-burning cook stove. In a few minutes it started squealing. My wife knew it needed something to eat. She took out the girls' doll bottle and filled it with milk, held the piglet in her arms, and fed it. After the first feeding it was fed every 3 hours by my wife. Each morning it was bathed with Ivory liquid soap. Its skin showed white with a pink tinge, hence, the piglet was named Pinky. Pinky had a special box to sleep, and was let out at times—Pinky's little hooves could be heard *click, click* on the hardwood floors.

Our girls claim that Pinky was the only pig that was put in a row boat and rowed or motored around the lake to be shown off or to play with the crowd of summer kids.

The rest of the story is sad. We overslept one Sunday morning. While Cora was feeding him, a gas bubble developed and he died in her arms.

—BEV RAND

WALKING HOME

I remember as a child, about 7 or 8 years old, walking with Heather Newman from my aunt Nessie's camp (Geneva Walker Start, whose camp is now owned by Richard and Barbara Burton). There was a walking path in front of all the camps. It was always such a thrill to walk that path knowing that all the strangers (to us) were happy and waving and always made us feel welcome!

—HEIDI HOLLIS RIGBY
Daughter of Bill and Connie Hollis

MY GREATEST FISHING DAY BIRTHDAY EXPERIENCE

The date was September 7, 1991, and the location was the salmon hole at Pleasant Pond, Island Falls, Maine. It was my 53rd birthday weekend. My birthday is on Sepetember 6. On that day, the weather was sunny, hot, humid, and the lake was completely calm, and no breeze. The fishing crew for the afternoon was Jean Edwards (the infamous fishing lady of the lake), my wife, Carolyn, my sister, Margaret, and her husband, Wally Gerow.

Enthusiasm for the afternoon's excursion on that extremely hot afternoon varied from Jean's, "We've got to get out there if we are going to catch anything" to Wally's, "You just don't catch salmon on a hot, calm day like this, believe me I know, but I'll go anyway."

So we nicely motored down the lake to one of Jean Edwards' special fishing spots at the well-known "salmon hole." Once the exact spot was located, per Jean's statement, "anywhere around here," the heavier-than-usual anchor was lowered.

I can't tell all the fishing secrets that Jean taught Carolyn and I over the years, but let me say that Jean started catching smelts for live bait to hopefully catch salmon.

For a half hour or so we exchanged a few fish stories, and Jean reminisced about the good old days when one could easily expect to catch a

▲ *Jean Edwards with her 5½-pound, 22-inch salmon caught while fishing with her friends Ted and Carolyn Roberts, on September 6, 1991, on Pleasant Pond (Courtesy of Ted Roberts)*

▲ *Wally's fish*
(Courtesy of Ted
Roberts)

salmon at will. We who fish for the great fish today know that it takes a great deal of patience and fortitude to wait out and pay your dues before you can expect to have bragging rights about catching one, let alone a large one. One year Carolyn and I fished diligently all one season and didn't catch a salmon. Wally attested to the fact that in years past the salmon population was very plentiful. *Now that you know the setting, let's get on with the story.*

Truthfully, I can't recall who caught the first salmon, but I'll try to account the sequence of events on that unforgettable fishing day. It seems that Wally started getting nibbles and the tip of his rod would go down just a bit, then pop up with a period of waiting. While we all were wondering if it was an eel or salmon, there would be another bob or two of the pole tip. Jean was really coaching Wally and told him to be ready to let line out. Guess what?! All of a sudden the tip of the pole sprang down to water's level and his reel was just a-singing. Wally hollered to Jean, "do I set the hook now?" Jean's reply was, "not yet, just wait until he stops and then wait for awhile until he has had a chance to eat the bait. I'll tell you when." She did and Wally got his catch of the day saying, "I can't believe I caught this salmon on a day like this!" This was fish number one and probably weighed 2½ pounds—nice fish.

Of course everyone was extremely excited in anticipation of what the next fish would weigh and who would catch it. The race was on, and everyone hurriedly put their lines back into the lake at or near the depth that Wally thought he caught his. There was a little chitchat and a lot of concentration as we watched for the little tapping that takes place on the end of the hook which is transmitted to the tip of the fishing pole. The tip of my pole bobbed a little, and then there wasn't anymore action. Patience is the name of game when you are trying to catch these sly specimens. After a short wait, another tap was observed. Again one must patiently wait, but I put a little line out to let the bait swim around at a different level to entice the biting fish. WOW!! All of a sudden I had a fish taking my line and I start paying line out ever so slowly as not to scare the fish from the bait, then waiting for the fish to tighten up on the bait before letting more line out. After waiting impatiently until I thought the fish had swallowed the bait fish, I set the hook, and then the fun began.

As I recall this fish made a great run out from the boat and jumped about 3 to 5 feet in the air and ran a couple more times jumping on each run.

Finally I was getting him close to the boat and hollered at Carolyn, "get the net." She hollered back, "I can't, I've just got a big fish on too." TOO HARD TO BELIEVE!! What now? Wally helped me by netting my salmon, and I in turn netted Carolyn's.

Both fish were between 3 and 4 pounds. Other salmon were caught, all over 2 and 3 pounds, within this feeding frenzy that lasted one-half to three-quarters of an hour. At one point three of us had a fish on at the same time! The best part of the story is yet to be revealed. OF COURSE BY THIS POINT WE THINK OUR FISHING DAY IS DONE.

As a matter of fact, Jean said, "yup, I guess that wraps up the fishing for today. You just don't catch that many fish and of that size and expect to catch more." However, we didn't need to coax her too much to keep fishing, since we only had been fishing a little over an hour. All lines went back into the fishing hole again!

All's quiet, and everyone was starting to get very hot on this calm, hot afternoon. I would say within 5 minutes of putting our lines out, Jean said, "I'm getting a nibble." Then, after a few more seconds, we saw the tip of her pole quickly dip two or three times and then *wham!*, her reel was singing and she hollered, "I've got a good one on!" She let the fish take the line, waited for it to stop and eat the bait, and then she set the hook. The fish immediately started a run, either going deep under the boat or out from the boat at breakneck speed.

All at once, Jean said, "I'm running out of line. What do I do?" I told her to keep the tip of her pole up, and grab the pole and line in her right hand to help slow down the fish's run. There was a lot of commotion in the boat with everyone hurrying to get their lines in so we wouldn't get tangled up with Jean's line. All at once we heard a real big splash nearly 200 feet from us on the other side of boat. I don't believe anyone saw it jump because we were expecting it to jump on Jean's side of the boat. We all anxiously turned to look at what was going on and then saw the fish on top of the water just warbling back and forth. We could see the dorsal fin and some of the top of the fish—like maybe it was getting its breath and resting. At this point we didn't know for sure if the fish was hooked or had broken loose from Jean's line. We were all looking in awe, wondering what was going to happen next. Wow, what a big fish!! What to do now?

Understand the situation now. Jean was on the port (left) side of the boat with her fly fishing rod that she always used, and a limp line. The fish had gone deep and under the boat and was coming out of the water some 200 feet on the starboard side of the boat. The question was, is the fish on? I told Jean to slowly reel in some line to see if the fish was on, which she did, ever so slowly, and the line finally came taught! Guess what now? The fish had been rejuvenating himself for another run and appeared to be heading towards the boat, leaving Jean's line slack. She said, "I can't reel fast enough," So I grabbed her line and started bringing it in hand over hand as fast as I could. We were now faced with a very precarious situation.

Physically I was bringing in Jean's line, but mentally I was thinking, how am I going to get the line around to Jean on the other side so she can bring in the fish? My dilemma was caused by the fact that we had a stringer of fish (20+ pounds) on the port side of the boat (Jean's side) an anchor line out with 70 or 80 feet of rope, and a heavy anchor on the end of it off the bow side, with an added concern about the propeller and I/O drive at the rear of the boat and still in the down position! WHAT TO DO?? AND QUICKLY TOO!! Someone responded to my excited yell to bring up the stringer of fish and drag it up over the side of the boat. Think about a 20-pound sack of potatoes in the water and how heavy it would be trying to anxiously and quickly lift it up out of the water and over the edge of the boat. Get the idea?

Now I was faced with the *anchor rope problem*. I quickly moved to the bow and put the fishing line in my mouth and started pulling the heavy anchor up hand over hand as fast as I possibly could. (I wonder now why I didn't have a heart attack), all the while with the fish line in my mouth. Thank God the fish wasn't pulling during all this activity. The fish must have been sulking on the bottom like some of the big ones do. I got the anchor in and asked Jean to come forward in the bow to have her start reeling in the slack—all the while telling her to keep the pole tip up. As I recall, we were both in the bow and Jean was just a little bit behind me and to my left. I think I still had the line in my mouth keeping it taught (I may have changed it to my hand now; I can't remember). Finally she had all the slack up and was ready to start bringing in the fish. Jean was so excited she could hardly think or keep her mind about her in anticipation of catching this big fish, not knowing for sure if it was a salmon, brook trout, or bass, or how big it was other than knowing it was big!! I recall I had to tell her repeatedly to keep her tip up. As a matter of fact, I think I actually reached out and pushed the pole up so the tip was up. She said, "Ted, please bring this fish in for me. I am too excited to do it!" I said, "no way, it's your fish!" ONE THING IS FOR SURE, WE HAD A BUSY, BUSY BOAT.

Jean finally got her wits about her and concentrated on bringing the fish in. The fish was exhausted from the deep and long runs it had made, thus coming in quite easily. Jean edged it to the side of the boat where I netted it after a couple of tries!

We had a thrash getting it out of the net and chasing it around in the boat. After all was said and done, we weighed it and the scales showed 5½ pounds. It was a beauty of a salmon. After taking stock of our catch we determined we had caught seven fish totaling 27 pounds—all within about an hour. As we sat there feeling quite pleased with ourselves, Jean commented that the salmon that she had just caught was the first one she had caught since we had upgraded to this larger boat. WE had been fishing from it for two or three years, and neither Carolyn nor I had ever noticed that she hadn't been catching salmon.

▼ *The seven fish (Courtesy of Ted Roberts)*

NOW THAT'S SOME FISH STORY!!! BUT I HAVE WITNESSES!!!

We were at our limit, overjoyed, and ecstatic as we headed up the lake. On the way we saw a friend of mine on his wharf, Gerald Clark, a former city manager for the City of Presque Isle, and we kind of swung in by his wharf area holding up the string of the seven fish. He hollered, "where in _____ did you catch all those salmon?" We just said quite nonchalantly, "down in the hole," as if we did it all the time.

Proceeding back to camp, we docked, laid out our catch on the picnic table, and took pictures for posterity. One picture that I gave to Jean (with Jean and her fish, or with her son Hollis, or both) ended up in Hollis's store in Hampden. A reporter saw it and asked if he could use it for an article he was writing about Jean. Of course Hollis said yes.

For the "And now you know the rest of the story," see the Appendix, an article from the Northwoods Sporting Journal titled "ON THE LAKE AGAIN" by Susan Morin. The pictures in the story are Jean with her fish, Wally with his fish, and the seven salmon laid out totaling a little over 27 pounds all caught within about an hour from one boat and five people, on September 7, 1991, a most wonderful day!! (The paper's article should have had the date being September 7, 1991, which is the date recorded in our camp log. And the weight of the fish was 5½ pounds.)

—TED ROBERTS

KALEIDOSCOPE

Dad hurriedly conducted us to his turquoise 1950 box car Buick for our first trip to Pleasant Pond. It was autumn 1960, and the frost had begun its annual slaughter of the leaves. Fallen and multicolored, the leaves were a blanket on the driveway and they swished as we kicked through them to the car. What a day! The air was so fresh and crisp that it hurt your lungs when you inhaled it. Everywhere the earthy smelling maples and oaks wore a coat of many colors amongst the minty evergreens.

We loped out of town and strained up the hill leaving the bone-white high school and elementary school buildings behind. As we crested the hill, all around us colors exploded. The tree-covered hills were alive with colorful music. Yellow, gold, bright red, and rusty child-like leaves danced cheerful ballets as they bravely dived from their stage and lightly floated on the breeze.

I instantly lost myself in their kaleidoscope, until I saw a diamond glint flash through the carousel of trees.

I kept pressing against the window anxiously watching as we drove along, and then the trees opened and there was Pleasant Pond, bluish white and shimmering. It was glimmering as a chilling breeze danced across its surface. Cold white soldier birches reverently guarded its shore, and the hill across the cove mirrored its own image on the surface of the water. The pond was simply beautiful, and there was a quiet patience about it that was very calming. When we exited the car and began exploring the camping area at Birch Point, I imagined the fun that summer would bring. My brothers were twins and nearly five years younger than me, which would make them about 8 years old at the time. They scampered here and there and were thoroughly enjoying their experience when Dad signaled that it was time to re-board. At the foot of the hill on the edge of the pond was Edwards' Birch Point Lodge. Dad took us inside and to our delight there was a small bowling alley, which seemed colossal. I still hear the thunder of the balls rolling down the alleys and the crack as they struck the candle pins. It was a place I spent many Saturdays throughout my school days. There was a camping area in the field and also amongst the birches, and there were small cabins to rent by the shore.

As autumn silently and almost imperceptibly crept away, the cold icy rains became a prelude to the frozen days of winter yet to come. By Thanksgiving that year the grass of the field was half hidden by a light crust of snow and seemed to desperately cling to life, as the color drained out. When the leaves left, there was a sorrow that hung over the ground like a shroud. Life just appeared to ebb away, and the jubilation of autumn gave way to the ugly starkness that lived between fall and winter.

One morning in early December, I awoke to a billowy blanket of quiet sleepy snow that had white washed the landscape. In winter, Pleasant Pond was girdled with cotton and often not a footprint nor a trail blemished the virgin snow. Sometimes the wind swished as it swept across the frozen crust, pushing the new snow across the pond in wisps and swirls. When the wind stopped, the silence was only broken by the occasional chattering of the squirrels scolding each other in the woods.

But, the quiet crept away and was replaced by the bustle of people skating in the cove or ice fishing. Though the cold was nearly paralyzing, the warmth inside the Birch Point Lodge or inside the ice fishing shan-

(Photo by Sandra Newman)

ties quickly warmed my numbed cheeks and toes until I felt like rubbing them off from the itching.

On skis, I shuffled across the pond suspended atop the snow trying not to break through and sink too deep. It made me a little nervous slipping my way along, wondering if there might be an opening in the ice beneath. I was careful, keeping watchful eyes scanning the way ahead. But every time I'd hear the ice crack or the snap of a brittle tree branch from the weight of the snow, I'd gasp.

When it seemed like winter would never end, the days began to lengthen, and the snow began to melt. The onset of spring was a process—snow melting, night falling, and water refreezing, and on and on the cycle turned, until there was mud and then the green began. April was a month for renewal, and the baby shoots struggled to climb out of their earthy cradle. Little purple, white, and blue flower children began appearing from their hiding places, and began to grow. After all, it was the '60s wasn't it?

Pleasant Pond was no small puddle; it was indeed a lake that seemed almost endless, encircled by an army of camps. But, because of the dense woods that hid the shoreline, unless you had a boat it was impossible to appreciate how many camps there were. We didn't have a boat during my years in Island Falls, so I never got to see all of Pleasant Pond. We mostly enjoyed swimming at Birch Point and having picnics there.

Summer was the lion of seasons and chased off the cowardly, young spring. The warmth of the sun forced the flowers to let go their young, and they scrambled forth to cover the meadows. There were so many types of flowers, Indian Pipes, Black-Eyed Susans, Daises, Forget-me-nots, Irises, and more.

We swam like fish, lingering in the water until we looked like our wrinkled flesh would fall off. We ate toasted marshmallows, roasted hot dogs, and grilled hamburgers until we thought we wouldn't live through the experience. As the evening sneaked upon us, the fireflies began their nightly dance and the bass frog choir croaked to us. It was a time to gaze upon the stars and wonder what it would be like to journey to them. What manner of life would we find? Were there other children like me gazing back and wondering those same thoughts?

Pleasant Pond had a power that caused you to dream and kindled your thoughts into a bonfire of expression. It was a place for all seasons, and I enjoyed my experiences not only during the years that I lived in Island Falls, but when I'd return. I'll never cease recalling the beauty of Pleasant Pond and the vivid memories that mean so much to me.

—JOEL T. ROBERTSON

LOVE AFFAIR WITH PLEASANT POND

I'm from Boston, and as children, my brother, Henry, and I would visit my grandparents, Bowman and Louise McLain, in Millinocket Maine. In 1948, we visited my Aunt Claudine and Uncle Owen who stayed in a camp by Wills Edwards. That began my love affair with Pleasant Pond and the people there. In 1950, I watched my grandfather and uncle clear the land in the cove and build Uncle Owen's camp, called Camp OBO for Owen and Bowman. Through the years many things change, but Pleasant Pond remains the same. I remember staying at Camp OBO and sleeping on the porch. On the weekend I would go to sleep to the music and sounds of happy people at the pavilion that has been replaced by music and laughter from the campers on the Point. As my family grew larger my husband, Robbie, my sons, Tony, Kevin Chris, and daughter, Jennifer, come and stay next door at Roberts' Camp-to-Come-to. We look forward to swimming, kayaking, fishing, and sleeping on the porch, listening to happy people on the Point—and let's not forget

Sand Cove. Tradition still carries on with our children and grandchildren, Kevin and Claire. Each year we enjoy the families next door and friends made through the years. There are times when we think about the 6 hour trip and contemplate not going, but Pleasant Pond and its people and the beautiful loons call back.

—PATTY MCLAIN ROBINSON

THE THINGS THAT WE SHARE (AND THE BIG FISH THAT DIDN'T GET AWAY)

This is our 15th summer spent at Birch Point. Ever since our oldest child learned how to walk, my wife and I decided that we'd spend as much time at the pond as possible. For the sheer beauty of this crystal clear lake nestled in between rolling hills of green hardwoods, we have fallen in love with the physical location that this unique place provides to our senses. For other reasons, for which I will explain later, it has become part of us, who we are as a family, and what we look forward to in the future.

My wife, Charlotte, my only daughter at the time, Jessica, and I came to visit some old friends at their family camp at the lower end of the lake in 1995. This camp was their destination so many years ago, before children, and even way before marriage! At the instant of first arriving for that visit, it seemed like a "Eureka" moment for Charlotte. Her childhood memories instantly came flooding back to her from long ago, when time seemed to stand still, and the summer days seemed so long. Then, having fun with her buddies was such an easy thing to do, without care, and without reservation. Here she was again at this very special place of her youth!

We arrived for that visit at Pleasant Pond with our new pop-up tent trailer, the one that we'd just travelled cross country in the year before, just me, Charlotte, and baby Jessica. We sure got a lot of travelling done, and out of our systems, during that adventure! In total we drove through twenty-six states, and visited nineteen national parks and monuments in a little over two months! Little did we realize at the time of visit to the lake that there would be a whole new way to enjoy our camper. As we spent the weekend parked in Tom and Erika's shorefront lot, enjoying our reunion with old friends, we caught sight of the campground that would soon become our seasonal destination for years to come.

Now that we were living in Bangor, the thought of bringing the camper up to Birch Point Campground for an extended stay seemed much more relaxing than what we had done the year before, with all the travelling. There was never a more perfect set of circumstances to capitalize on a new idea—we had friends in the area, Charlotte loved the lake, we owned a nifty camper, and the campground was just down the road! Later that summer we came up for several weeks during a vacation, and we were sold—hook, line, and sinker!

Every year since, we've enjoyed the same Campsite #6 for the entire summer season, and sometimes beyond. We are now a family of five, with daughter Jessica turning 16, daughter Samantha turning 13, and our little prince, Anthony, who is turning 7 years old. Charlotte and I are proud that our children know very little else of what a summer's vacation should be for them, than spending the entire season at Birch Point. It is where many memories have been made, as well as many lasting friendships.

▼ *Powers Point (Photo by Sandra Newman)*

Our site is a very special one, easily recognized by any of us as the spot on the Point. It is not because of the nice mix of sun and shade it offers with its big bunch of birch trees, or for the perfect little spot that we set up our camper, which allows for beautiful lake views from our front door. Our site has become a real "home" for us, situated within a string of similar seasonal "homes" occupied by great summertime neighbors, fine "county folks" that anyone could possibly or have as friends. Since we first occupied our special spot that first summer, we've shared our growing family with the same group of families over the years, with little variation, each summer, for the past fifteen years. For no small reason that we find such pleasure in staying at Birch Point, than also spending the entire season among the Ganleys, the McAvoys, the Larabees, the Collins, the Clarks, and of course, the Edwards. This is what makes this place so special to us. It is no longer just for the sheer beauty of the location that we find it so attractive.

Over the years we've shared plenty. It's hard to believe that Brandon was only 6 when we first came to Birch Point, and now he's an upper classman at Maine Maritime Academy, and fixing our cars! We've seen young girls grow up to be beautiful brides, some having of their own, making proud grandparents of our peers. We've been to weddings, and unfortunately some funerals also. There's been good news and not-so-good-news, and yet it is shared in easy conversation among friends, around a campfire, or the radio's Red Sox game, and usually with some liquid refreshment to go along with it. It is within this close-knit neighborhood of friendship, one in which each "front dooryard" looks into the others, that I want to retell my story of our little Anthony's big moment this summer.

Certainly Anthony was in the right place, at the right time, and more than just once, for he and Mike to share such a memory. It was a day in mid-June, soon after school let out, and the whole summer laid out in front of us for another splendid season. Anthony had never been asked to go on Mike's boat to go fishing before, but he always admired that sleek, black boat, with a matching black Mercury motor and gray canvas cockpit. When the invitation came unexpectedly, he took it just like a fish to bait. Mike always wanted to turn a kid on to fishing, and he figured he had got a good prospect in Anthony that day. They were both excited.

It was mid-afternoon and the day was still sunny, which was a rare event for that month. As usual, Mike motored to the far end of the lake

▼ *Anthony's 3+ pound, 20-inch salmon (Courtesy of Anthony Sardina)*

where the water is 60-inches deep by Barker Rocks. There, he helped his little friend bait his hook with a shiner and showed Anthony how to plug for the big fish way down deep. They were hoping for something substantial, like a salmon or a trout. (Back at the campsite, both Charlotte, and Mike's wife, Linda, hoped and prayed that the boys would come home with a trophy fish.)

About an hour or so into their adventure, Anthony was looking a bit bored for the lack of any bites on their lines, so Mike thought that maybe they'd head back to camp and try again some other day. He was getting the boat ready for the return trip up the lake, when Anthony said to Mike, "Hey, I think something's wrong with my fishing pole!" When Mike turned to look, Anthony's pole was bent right over and had he not quickly helped him to steady it, it may have soon been out of his little hands and into the lake. At first he thought that Anthony may have hooked something on the bottom, but with the pole steadied in Anthony's hands he felt the quickening of the line with Anthony's very first fish at the other end. Now they were really excited.

Mike was sure to let Anthony do all the work of reeling in his catch. It took a while, maybe 10 minutes, but the fish finally came to the surface, and Mike thought that it had jumped out of the water about five times on its way to the side of the boat. (Anthony recollects that it was only four.) With his arms sore from the fight, Anthony let Mike net his first fish, to find out that he landed a 20-inch salmon weighing over 3 pounds! At this point, Mike's enthusiasm was even greater than Anthony's, as the little fella didn't even realize what a tremendous catch it was—not only that it was the first time he had ever dipped a line for one! They each gave the other a high five and headed home to tell the good news. Linda got the call from Mike's cell phone that Anthony caught the only fish that trip and that they were due back in a few minutes. Charlotte and Linda counted their blessings that such a memory could be made in such a small amount of time.

When they arrived at Mike's dock, Anthony was the proud storyteller of the day's event, yet his enthusiasm barely matched that of Mike's, who had taken many young boys out for their first fishing trip over the years but never had the opportunity to tell such a big fish story himself. Never, could he imagine he said, that a pole could be bent over as far as Anthony's without the little fella going overboard with it! As I was working in Bangor that day, I got a voicemail on my own cell phone from

Anthony that I hope to keep forever. He was so proud to have caught his first fish and wanted me to know about it right away. Sister Jessica was on hand to take the photo of Anthony and Mike with the big one that didn't get away, and to show these boys with the most satisfied smiles across their faces.

This is a recent example of how the world can become a real small place, in Island Falls, Maine. A place that is shared amongst ourselves and with each other in a way that spans generations, it seems, and gives great pleasures—both big and small—to those who simply want to enjoy the good life. We love it here and will always come back. It's our home away from home, thanks to such nice people as we've come to know at Birch Point Campground.

"I'd like to thank the entire Edwards Family for providing us the opportunity to enjoy Birch Point Campground and Pleasant Pond over these many years, as well as many more in the future."

—JOE AND CHARLOTTE SARDINA

A BIRCH POINT CHILDHOOD

▼ *Roger Tuft, 1996 (Courtesy of Roger Tuft)*

"Biiiiiig Boat." My first enthusiastic attempt at a sentence was spoken in a tiny cabin at Birch Point on Pleasant Lake. Sitting on Cabin #7's splintery dock three summers later, with legs barely long enough to hang over the edge, I watched as the boats, still big by my standards, hurried past me. Perched there amongst my collection of rocks and bugs, I dreamed of the day it would be my turn to experience an adventure on a "big boat."

Hearing my name, I raced down to the shore and joined my grandfather in his boat. A confident swimmer at 7 years old, I was finally deemed ready to learn how to fish on the pond! Bumping and splashing our metal craft over the whitecaps, we gradually slowed and eased into our chosen spot under the power lines. Handing my grandfather his rod, he expertly showed me the reel's trigger, the cast, and how to guide the lure into the lake. Grabbing my rod and pulling it back, I swung it around with a whoosh, trying to get as much distance as possible. My awkward attempts that followed were eventually successful. There we sat, grandfather and grandson, waiting and waiting for the fish to bite. Squirming and fidgeting, I tried in vain to get comfortable in the boat. Occupying my mind with the sights and sounds around me, the mountain foliage and picturesque view of the Lane Farmhouse mirrored in the water, a distant loon diving for food, and the waves from our wake hitting the shore, I found some quiet within myself. I was learning patience. At last, feeling a tug on my line, I wrestled in my first catch. It was then my grandfather announced that I was a *true man*.

At the same lake in Maine almost ten years later, so much in my life has changed. Standing in a new log cabin built by my family, I gaze at the many photos on the wall of the past seventeen summers. On the dresser, a framed picture of myself as an infant being bathed in a shallow sink of Birch Point's Cabin #7 fills me with a sense of belonging. These memories truly are the pivotal moments of my childhood; cooking s'mores on blazing campfires, Labrador retrievers leaping off of the dock, and grand flotillas of inner tubes loaded down with siblings and cousins headed for Mildred Edwards' float. I come to the realization of what this lake means to me. As my family's gathering place, this is where I have learned my role in this family. It is also where my development as an individual began. Here, I became a part of the bigger picture of life. I formed a healthy respect for the simplicity of the outdoors. Island Falls, Maine, is where I spoke those first words, where I acquired patience, and where I started to become this true man of whom my grandfather spoke. Nurtured by these many summers at Pleasant Lake, I am forever grateful for my childhood. And like that child, I will always be eager for the experience of adventure, the opportunity to learn, and the promise of the future.

—ROGER TUFTS

THE TWILIGHT ZONE

(Bebe and Susie Hunt, at an early age, were walking from the Point to their camp on Pleasant Pond.)

We were walking along the road from Birch Point, and just before Crabtree Lane we saw an old fashion buckboard on its side down in the woods, and we could see the wooden spokes. We were so excited, we decided to run back to camp to get our brother, Pat, and cousin, Frank O'Brian, for help pulling it out. It must have been there a long time; there were bushes growing around the wheels and up over the flat bed.

The troop arrived to salvage the beast, but lo and behold the buckboard was nowhere to be found! Susie and I searched and searched, we pushed down bushes, and we trampled in the muck, wondering if someone found it just before us. We have never found the buckboard or its remains.

To this day, Susie admits she still looks for it whenever she walks by the spot on the Pond Road. The Twilight Zone, possible time warp, or whatever it was—we know what we saw over fifty years ago.

—BEBE (HUNT) WALKER

CHAPTER 9

Trivia

BASIC POND FACTS THAT *MIGHT* BE TRUE

Pleasant Pond is referred to as a pond because it has only an outlet and no inlet. With only very fresh spring water as its water source, it can often be freezing cold. You may have discovered this fact while swimming or falling while water skiing. Once you hit a spring you know without a doubt the difference between spring-fed ponds and lakes with tributaries.

+ Pleasant Pond is 5 miles long and 1 mile wide, with depths ranging between 60 to 65 feet at the lower end, and 25 to 40 feet at the upper end.
+ Mr. Dick Albright reported catching 101 salmon when ice fishing during the winter of 2009. He records the number of fish for the Maine Fish and Game, and in return receives the most beautiful wildlife watercolors painted by various Maine artists.
+ All spring fed, you can see the bottom easily at depths up to 25 to 30 feet.
+ The Powers own around 11,000 acres at the end of the pond, saving our beautiful pond from further development!
+ The Island Falls' town line is 200- to 300-feet below the Pond Road: the pond is in Island Falls, the top side of the road is Dyer Brook.
+ Dyer Brook maintains the road for people living in Island Falls.
+ Everybody living close to the road or within 200-feet downhill from the road live in Dyer Brook. Close to the water, you live in Island Falls.
+ Clara Hathaway is the oldest living person who danced in the Birch Point Pavilion. When it was originally built, Clara was 17 years old. This year, 2010, she celebrates her 103rd birthday.
+ The Crabtree and Hillman camps are two of the oldest on the pond.

+ The sawmill, built at the head of the pond in 1939, maintained business for four years.
+ Richard Armstrong and Jerry Bradbury had the only private planes on the pond.
+ The Palmers had one of the first sailboats.
+ Dr. Swett and Jacob Shur had the first power boats.
+ Nels Martin had the one and only houseboat.
+ The cute, little yellow cottage next to Birch Point Lodge, the Tingley Cottage, was the Walker-Edwards-Lane School and might be the oldest building on the pond.
+ Swimming lessons were held at Birch Point, Sand Cove, and Swett's Cove.
+ Bean-hole Beans are offered every Saturday night at Birch Point, a tradition that was started by W. F. Edwards in 1925.
+ Raymond Michaud made the best raspberry pie, serving it with a large scoop of French vanilla ice cream. He made the pies daily from the berries he picked early in the morning in the raspberry patch where the laundry building is today. He always remembered to stuff each pie with more than enough fruit; you had to order your piece early, because no matter how many he had, the dining room always ran out.
+ Lib Harmon, Pat Emerson, Charlie Walker, Larry and Anne Tompkins, Reneva Jones Smith, Phil Faulkner, Sally (Walker) Cyr, Sandy Newman, and Mike Corveau were among the swimming instructors at Birch Point.
+ There are 157 lots on the pond.
+ There was a dam built at the lower end around 1898.
+ There are 65 Birch Point campsites and 10 cottages.
+ There are 10 Camp Theodore Roosevelt cottages and one formerly in Pratt's Cove, Mattawamkeag Lake.
+ The restaurant at Birch Point is The Trail's End: (207) 463-2515
+ The restaurant at Va-Jo-Wa is Craig's Maine Course: (207) 463-2128
+ Camp Theodore Roosevelt: (207) 463-2191
+ For all you walkers and runners, distances on Pond Road from Birch Point:
  – 1.0 miles to the Va-Jo-Wa Golf Course turn-off with up and down rolling hills!

- 1.7 miles to Va-Jo-Wa Golf Course, up more hills and around a few turns
- 1.3 miles to the Main Road (U.S. Route 2) with even more ups and downs, and a few more turns
- 1 mile from Birch Point to Lane Homestead going right at top of Birch Point Hill encountering sort of rolling hills
- 2.4 miles from Main Road (U.S. Route 2) to Lane Homestead

Enjoy whatever you might stumble upon!

◄ *Bill and Connie (Walker) Hollis Cabin welcome plaque (Photo by Sandra Newman)*

Appendix

On the Lake again.....

By Susan Morin, Northwoods Sporting Journal

Jean Edwards of Island Falls, Maine just recently turned 75 years old and has not lost her zeal for fishing. This lady starts her fishing at ice-out and is still fishing long into September each year.

The photo above shows Jean with her 5 lb., 22 inch Salmon caught while fishing with her friends Ted and Caroline Roberts on September 6, 1992 on Pleasant Pond in Island Pond, Maine. Five other people caught Salmon that day in the range of 2-5 lbs. Jean has been fishing on Pleasant Pond since 1947.

" I practically brought my kids up on the lake, I was always fishing." she chuckled.

Her children, Hollis Edwards, who now owns Aunt Mary's Country Store and resides in Winterport and Lea Downs of Milford were probably seen many a day out fishing with Mom where they acquired irreplaceable memories. What a great way to spend time with Mom!

When her kids grew up Jean needed a new fishing "buddy". Her grandson, Seth Edwards, of Milford fit the bill.

When asked how young she started taking Seth out fishing Jean stated, "Soon as he wasn't afraid of the motor."

Seth is now 18 years old and is graduating this June and still refers to his Gram as "his fishing buddy".

Many times he'll call up his Gram and say,"Hey how'd you like to go out fishing with your "old fishing buddy" today."

Another generation of memories being passed down... I wonder how soon Seth will start his children fishing? Soon as they're not afraid of the motor? My guess is probably just about the time they can grip a fly rod.

"Many times he'll call up his Gram and say,"Hey, how'd you like to go out fishing with your "old fishing buddy today?"

Jean has kept records for over 25 years for biologist. Every year she is sent a book that diagrams different areas of fin clips. Where that clip is made on the Salmon determines the year that fish was stocked. She records every fish that is caught with a fin clip and by the diagrams she can give it the year it was stocked.

Every day this lady starts off on another day of fishing she records starting time, time ended, how many caught, date size and length and also "the ones that got away! Fish and Game acknowledged her years of service by presenting her with two limited edition prints by Maine artists.

In the 1960's Jean was written up by Bud Leavitt of the Bangor Daily News for catching over 60 Salmon that year with the biggest being 6 pounds. Many people had an interest in what she was using.

She said ."Folks thought she must have been using the "right thing" to catch that many." Jean's pretty sure it was an American Beauty that did the trick that year.

"Wasn't too long ago you could catch up to 7 1/2 pounds of Salmon a day, that sure was a lot of fun!"

You probably would like a clue as to what our lady fisherman uses for her favorite lures and flies, I know I would! She agreed to satisfy our curiousity "somewhat" by revealing that she always uses fly rod and fly line and a few of her favorites but...she is not willing to share her favorite spots on Pleasant Pond. Can't say that I blame her!

Her favorite streamer flies; Tandem hook Mickey Finn and Nine-Three and her favorite lure; Blaze Orange Mini Super Duper.

In conclusion, after speaking with Jean she summed up the soul of a fisherman. As with most fisherman it's not the size of the catch, or the number of fish but what it evokes and awakens in each of us.

This great lady told me, "I never feel cheated if I've spent all day fishing and haven't gotten a fish or even a hit because I've spent the day surrounded by the mountains, on a beautiful lake and no matter how many times I go out I notice something I hadn't seen the last time or something will seem more beautiful than it ever did before."

We also want to thank our "Roving Salesman", Lionel Strong of Enfield for spotting this great picture at Aunt Mary's Country Store in Hampden. He suggested that it might make a great picture and story for the Northwoods Sporting Journal. He was right! Thanks Lionel for making a special trip to Hampden last week to make sure we had the picture in time for deadline!

▼ *Original Birch Point Log Camps brochure*

BIRCH POINT LOG CAMPS

Pleasant Lake
Island Falls, Maine

The place to hunt and fish, to boat and swim. The place to play and rest. . . .

BIRCH POINT
On Katahdin Scenic Trail

On the shore of Pleasant Lake
With a million fish to take
Is a little paradise
Right above your eyes
Under cloudless skies
So blue.

It's a beauty spot of Maine
Birch Poi—n—t is it's name
Nestled in the hills
Not a lot of frills
But, a thousand thrills
For you.

Mt. Edwards is the Prop,
And you'll find that he's tip top
Cosy cabins, nice and clean
Finest food you've ever seen
Everything is so serene
It's home.

When it's time to get a deer
You will find him waiting here
Up some winding, wooded trail
In a pleasant little vale
You will see an old "white tail"
Your own.

When the lure of nature calls
Take the road to Island Falls
Then a drive of four short miles
Bill will greet you with a smile
Settle down and rest awhile
It's home.

Ernest B. Southard.

1935?

Birch Point Log Camps

COME BY AUTO, PLANE OR TRAIN

From Portland take Route 1 to Bangor or 100 to Augusta, 201 to Waterville, and 100 to Pittsfield, then 2 to Bangor and Island Falls. From Bangor to Island Falls it is 100 miles over fine roads of macadam and tarvia.

ACCOMMODATIONS ARE TRULY FINE

There are 7 splendid log camps and 5 overnight cabins— clean, comfortable quarters; electric lights, good beds; cold, clear water from boiling springs; and best of food, palatably presented, fresh from lake, stream and farm. Tennis court, boats and canoes are at your disposal. Registered guides, courteous and amicable, will escort you if you desire.

Rates

$3.00 per day — boats and canoes included

Weekly Rates on Request

Stop at ISLAND FALLS HARDWARE CO.
for Tourist Information

Our hunting camp is located in some of the finest hunting country in Maine. Bear, deer and partridge are plentiful. The deer pictures above were shot during the 1935 hunting season.

The buck shown below was one of several fine specimens taken during the 1934 season.

▼ *Original Birch Point Log*
Camps brochure

Maine is Nature at her Best

Our Log Camps face beautiful Pleasant Lake. Meals may be had at the central dining camp. Some of the camps are equipped for preparing meals.

Boats and canoes are on hand for the use of the campers. There are excellent swimming facilities at a nice gravel beach.

Congenial guides are always available for hunting, fishing or hiking parties.

Good Fishing

Reaching an occasional depth of 75 feet, fed almost entirely by its own boiling springs, Pleasant Lake, five miles long by one wide, offers tourists, especially just after the ice goes out, some of the finest salmon and trout fishing in the State. Generously stocked each season.

All Roosevelt's Hunting Country

The region about Island Falls has long been famous as excellent country for Deer, Bear, Bobcat, Partridge and Duck shooting. Around Mattawamkeag Lake, where Roosevelt spent most of his time, is a very noted game country.

Come to

BIRCH POINT CAMPS
Island Falls, Maine

Many Waters for Fishing

Mattawamkeag Lake abounds with Black Bass, Perch, Pickerel, Trout and Salmon; is well stocked with Salmon each year. Its tributaries, all good trout waters, are Mud Lake, Rockabema Lake, West Branch of the Mattawamkeag River, Alder Brook, Cold Brook, Fish Stream, Crystal Brook, Dyer Brook, Sly Brook, and Bog Brook. These all readily accessible and most of them right in the heart of Island Falls.

The Hunting Lodge—This camp is on the bank of the East Branch of the Mattawamkeag River, three miles deep in the forest.

In summer it is the resting place or overnight stop for fishing parties or hikers. In the hunting season it is used by hunting parties who return each year to bag their quota of partridge and deer.

▼ *Original Fisher's Log*
   Lodge brochure

• PLEASANT LAKE •

Pleasant Lake is one of Maine's best fishing waters. The size, quantity, and quality are superior to many other highly rated lakes. The water is crystal clear and nearly 100% pure drinking, making the fish caught of highest quality.

There are the small mouth scrappy bass, salmon and brown trout, also, white perch and smelts. When the fish are slow in biting, one may go to one of the other nearby lakes or streams. Namely:

Mattawamkeag L. — bass, pickerel, perch. 10 minutes from camp.

Skiticook L. — white perch, pickerel, about 15 mins. from camp.

Timoney L. — beautiful speckled trout. 10 min. from camp.

Spaulding L. — perch, trout, salmon. 10 min. from camp.

East Branch River — trout. 5 minutes from camp.

The services of registered guides who know this territory are available. Licenses can be obtained here on the lake.

Area Abounds In Deer

Fisher's Log Lodges are easy to reach by auto. However, if you have trouble call u and we'll direct you.

The Gateway to ...
FISHING AND HUNTING
Aroostook County, Maine
Fisher's Log Lodge
and
LOG CABINS

Pleasant Lake	—	Maine's Finest
Island Falls		Tel. 31-31

One of Fisher's Log Cabins

Aroostook County, Maine is better than average Hunting country and Island Falls area is quite centrally located. There are thousands of acres of cut-over timberland clearing with tote roads making it ideal hunting ground. More than 1800 deer are tagged each season in this area. Many partridge are taken in this section, too. Also ducks.

Black bears are numerous here. This crafty animal when startled will go through the woods at terrific speed making it rather difficult to "draw a bead" quickly.

▼ *Original Fisher's Log
Lodge brochure*

Fisher's Log Lodges are in the Heart of Maine's Best Recreation Area

100 Miles North of Bangor
Turn left at Macwahoc

Recreation: Many summer people who come to play and relax, other than fishing find enjoyment in visiting other sections. Mt. Katahdin, about a 3 hour drive, affords mountain climbing and beautiful scenery. There are many picnic areas.

Houlton Community Golf Course offers a nice place for ardent golfers. It has a sporty nine-hole, par 36 course on well-kept greens, bordering Nickerson Lake, about a half hour from camp.

Swimming is enjoyed by all at Fisher's Lodge. A good beach and wharfs make it ideal for bathers who do not swim much. There are no "drop offs" and because of the clear water, one can see bottom at all times.

Island Falls is a typical New England village with the usual grocery stores, a

drug store, hardware and sporting goods store. There is a hospital, three or four churches, and restaurant serving excellent food. There is, also, a very nice dining room right on the lake about

Mr. Fisher shown with a Pleasant Lake salmon. 5 minutes from camp.

CLEAN AND SPACIOUS

We have a clean, quiet and attractive place which the guests appreciate. Repeat business is our best recommendation. Make reservations early because of our limited accommodations. The Lodge can take care of guests whenever necessary.

The cabins are modern with running water, flushes, lavatories, etc. They are equipped for light housekeeping with gas for cooking. Linen, dishes, etc. are furnished. In the summer, those who wish to eat out may do so at a very nice dining room right on the lake about five minutes from camp. During Hunting season, arrangements may be made at the Lodge for meals.

Cabins Nos. 1, 2, and 3 are all $12 per day for two, three or four people, respectively, or, $75 per week if they stay two weeks. Cabin No. 3 has two bedrooms.

Come to Fisher's ... You'll Be Glad You Came

▼ *Original Camp Theodore Roosevelt brochure*

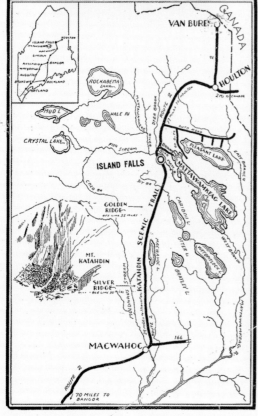

Camp
Theodore Roosevelt
HOUSEKEEPING CABINS

In the Maine woods
On beautiful Pleasant Lake

AROOSTOOK COUNTY
ISLAND FALLS, MAINE

F. JOSEPH McAULIFFE, Owner

Established 1923

▼ *Original Camp Theodore Roosevelt brochure*

THE MAINE WOODS CALL YOU TO CAMP THEODORE ROOSEVELT

*S*PEND a glorious vacation at Camp Theodore Roosevelt in famous Aroostook County. Here the Maine Woods call you to Pleasant and Matta-wamkeag Lakes to wet a line for scrappy black bass. Come and enjoy perfect relaxation and comfort at our main set of cabins on the shore of beautiful Pleasant Lake.

All housekeeping cabins at Pleasant Lake are equipped with blankets, bed linen (weekly), towels (daily), two-burner gas plates, running water, wood heater stoves, cooking utensils, china, silverware, and ice refrigerators. Community shower. Some cabins have flush toilets; others, chemical.

Catholic and Protestant churches in the village.

Camp Roosevelt is located on Pleasant Lake, a beautiful body of water five miles long and nearly surrounded by an unbroken forest. A road runs direct to camp from Route 2

SUGGESTIONS FOR YOUR OUTFIT

Camera, fishing tackle, flashlight, rubbers, rain-coat, heavy sweater, woolen socks for hiking, khaki trousers and shirts, old hat, extra pair of old shoes, bathing trunks.

For the women folk: Slacks and shorts, afternoon dress for dances at Birch Point, FLAT heel footwear, socks, swim suit.

Bass Fishing in Pleasant Lake

Have three-pound pull and a five-pound bite,
An eight-pound jump and a ten-pound fight,
A twelve-pound bend to your rod,-but alas!
When you get him aboard, he's a half-pound bass."

Pleasant Lake is five miles long by one and a half miles wide. It is spring fed and crystal clear. The shores, lined in many places with large rocks, gradually slope to a depth of ten and drop off to twenty feet of water. It is along this drop-off that the bass hang out and are taken with artificial flies or live bait, such as grasshoppers, worms, small frogs, and hellgrammites. Maribou streamer flies and Flat-fish are effective.

Hellgrammites cannot be obtained at camp.

Bass, Pickerel, and White Perch in Lake Mattawamkeag

Mattawamkeag Lake is eight miles long by three at its widest. It abounds in weedy coves, rocky and sandy shores. Here the bass bite best on such plugs as the pikie minnow, river runt spook, and bass oreno. In August small frogs fished off the weed beds in this lake are very effective. Pickerel fishing is good on cloudy days and the white perch are great fun at sundown. Camp Roosevelt has a housekeep-ing cabin four miles by boat down Mattawamkeag for those who like to rough it a bit and enjoy unsur-passed fishing for bass, pickerel, and white perch.

For fishing with live bait a short shank, size 2/0, gut hook is best.

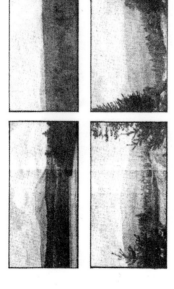

WELCOME TO ISLAND FALLS, MAINE... A SPORTS LOVER'S SHANGRI-LA

In the whole of Aroostook County there is no more picturesque town than Island Falls and none where the natural beauty is more awe inspiring. It is a sportsman's paradise and is noted as a pleasant, healthy, and beautiful summer resort. Its lakes, rivers, and wooded hills add much to the attractiveness of the town, and nowhere is there a purer air, or a more comfortable summer temperature than here.

The west branch of Mattawamkeag River enters the town near the northwest corner and, after flowing south for nearly two miles and being enlarged by the confluence of Fish Stream, sweeps madly through a rocky gorge and dashes over precipitous ledges, forming one of the finest falls in the country! Midway of the falls is a small island, its rocky sides rising abruptly from the water and dividing the swift current. This little wooded island in the midst of the falls gives the name to the town of Island Falls. After leaping the falls the river continues in a course a little south of east for nearly three miles, when it empties into Mattawamkeag Lake, a beautiful body of water which covers a large portion of the eastern part of the town.

Previous to 1842, no white man had pitched his habitation in this picturesque region. Indians from the Penobscot and Passamaquoddy tribes were accustomed to spend a part of the year hunting and fishing in this vicinity and had their camps near the falls. The Island Falls area also possesses spectacular Pleasant and Mattawamkeag Lakes. President Theodore Roosevelt camped on Mattawamkeag Lake and used Island Falls as his summer home. Pleasant Lake is one of the few spring-fed lakes in Maine, and possesses crystal-clear water. It is famous for its spring salmon fishing, while Mattawamkeag Lake is renown for its bass, pickerel, and perch fishing, as well as the good hunting along its shore and camping areas.

The area around Island Falls also contains many other lakes, streams, rivers, and brooks and is only 40 miles from famous Baxter State Park, a 200,000-acre state park in which spectacular Mount Katahdin is located, the highest peak in the State of Maine and the end of the famous Appalachian Trail.

The village of Island Falls supports a nine and "soon to be completed" eighteen-hole golf course, a time-share condominium resort, a well-maintained camping area, and all the amenities of modern living including a well-staffed medical center and shopping areas.

Bangor International Airport is only 85 miles south of Island Falls, and Boston is approximately 330 miles.

We at United National Real Estate are proud to be a part of such a beautiful community. Our professional staff will save you time and money in your search for that perfect real estate value-- whether it is a farm, retreat, country estate, home or business opportunity.

Contributing
Memories and Stories

Dottie (Alford) Martin

Bruce Boisvert, Candy (Byron) Guerette

Patti (Desmond) Hartin, Jane (Dow) Fitzgerald

Joe Edwards, Steven Edwards, Sherry (Edwards) Hosford, Pat Emerson

Wallace A. Gerow, Alexis Glidden, Cindy and Richard Gray

Darlene Hartin, Clara Hathaway, Pamla (HIllman) Oliver

Marion Hoar, Sharman (Hoar Drew) Ball, Heidi (Hollis) Rigby, Patrick
    Hunt, Bebe (Hunt) Walker

Ava Joy, Becky (Joy) Drew

Bruce Larlee, Gayleen Leavitt

Joe and Susie McAuliffe, Joanie (McAuliffe) Walsh

Jennifer (McGraw) McCourt, Bob McCaffrey

Patty (McLain) Robinson, Mark Robinson

Dr. Ray C. Newman

Jane A. Packer, Mary (Packer) Ardizzone, Doris Pankratz

Ralph and Valerie (Lake) Powers, Philip and Averill Powers

Ed Quinlan

Bev Rand, Ted Roberts, Mark Robertson, Joel T. Robertson

Joe and Charlotte Sardina, Roger Tuft

Francis and Sally (Walker) Cyr, Bill and Connie (Walker) Hollis

Winnie (White) Desmond

Resources

Burleigh. "Island Falls Plantation." Map. *Maine State Archives.* Augusta, Maine, 1877.

Drew, Rebecca (Joy). Librarian. Raw data. Katahdin Public Library, Island Falls, ME. Summer 2009.

Drew, Rebecca (Joy). Historian. *Pleasant Pond Photographs.* Island Falls Historical Society, Pleasant Pond, Island Falls, ME.

"Highway Map." Map. *Prentiss & Carlisle Co. Inc Surveys.* Bangor, ME. 1935.

"Island Falls, ME. Topographic Map." *Customized Topo Map.* 2009.

Maps and Pond Information. Raw data. Island Falls Town Office, Island Falls, ME. Aug.

Newman, Sandra S. *Pleasant Pond Photographs.* Summer 2009. Sandy's Pleasant Pond Collection, Pleasant Pond, Island Falls, ME.

Raw data. Houlton Registry of Deeds, Houlton, ME. Aug. 2009.

Raw data. Maine State Archives, Augusta, Maine. Aug. 2009.

Raw data. Stories submitted from People Living on Pleasant Pond. 2009.

Bibliography

Edwards, Keith. Memories of Keith Edwards. Raw data. Pleasant Pond, Dyer Brook, Maine.

Edwards, Ralph R. History of Pleasant Lake. Raw data. Pleasant Pond, Dyer Brook, Maine.

Gilman, George H., ed. "Houlton in Spring of 1895." *Publishing Aroostook Pioneer Illustrated Souvenir Edition.*

Haskell, B. "Maine Resort Industry's Undiscovered Giant." *Bangor Daily News.* 17 July 1982: pg. 18.

"Joe Edwards and His Pleasant Pond Memories." Personal interview. Summer 2009.

King, April. "The Burleigh Family of Linneus." *Burleigh Genealogies,* pg. 15.

Lincoln, President Abraham. "Homestead Act of 1862." *Library of Congress.* Rpt. in *American Memory.*

"Llewellyn Powers." *Wikipedia.*

"One-Room School." *Wikipedia.*

Sawyer, Nina G. *The History of Island Falls—1843–1972.* Caribou, ME: Custom Printers, 1972.

Smith, Dr. Alan. *Remembrances of Versailles High School.* Versailles: Ripley, IN.

Wiggin, Edwards. *History of Aroostook.* Vol. 1. Presque Isle, ME: The Star Herald Press, 1922.

Sandy with her mom, Joy (Skinner) Newman (Photo by Tim Hathaway)

Sandy with her dad, Dr. R. C. Newman—Islands Falls' veterinarian for sixty years (Photo by Tim Hathaway)

My interests became studies. My studies became transportation. My transportation became adventures. My adventures became stories. My stories became the interest of others.

—SANDY NEWMAN

About the Author

Sandra Newman grew up in the small northern Maine town of Island Falls and spent her summers with other "pond kids," swimming in the wicked-cold water of Pleasant Pond. With her friends, Sandy enjoyed leisurely, fun-filled days, and she was rarely seen out of her swimsuit, except when sleeping or for the proverbial trip to town. She survived on macaroni salads, forever sunshine, and water-skiing. What more could a "pond kid" ask for?

It was while living in New Mexico, working as a tour director and Rocky Mountain Ski Instructor, that Sandy discovered storytelling. She loved entertaining eager listeners with her sharp, quick-witted stories about her hometown, Island Falls, the town's local residents, and life on the pond. When a friend whose family was among the first settlers on Pleasant Pond asked her to tell his story, she happily agreed. This is the pond's story. Enjoy!

▲ *A Perfect Morning (Photo by Sandra Newman)*

To live as fully, as completely as possible, to be happy is the true aim and end to life.

—LLEWELLYN POWERS